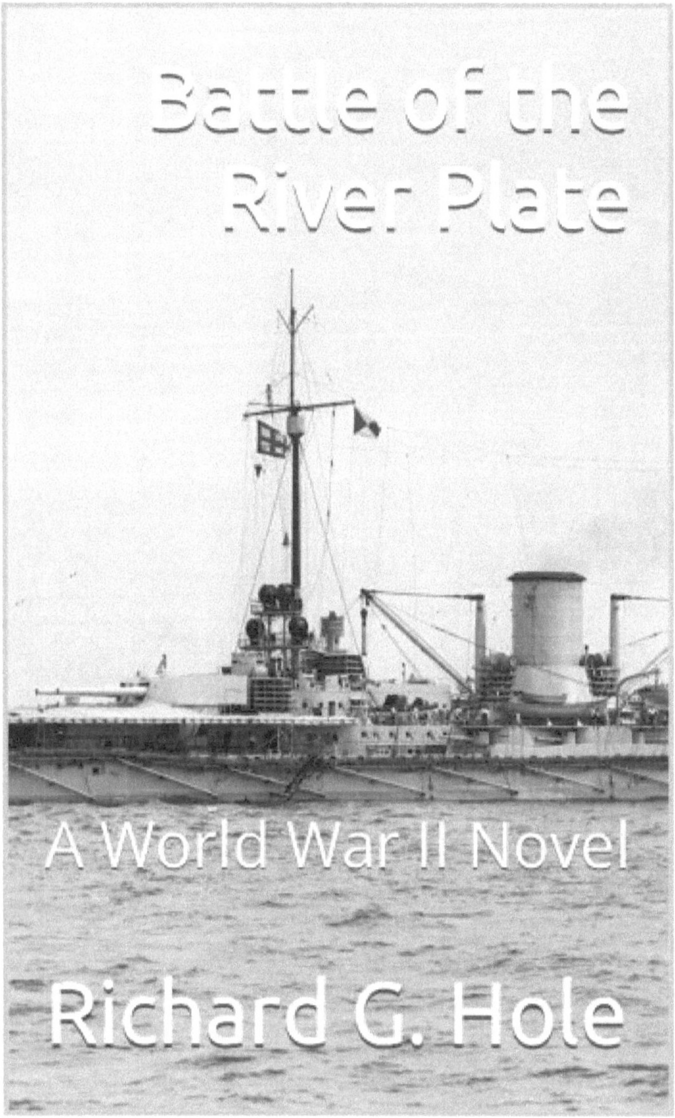

Battle of the River Plate

A World War II Novel

Richard G. Hole

Battle of the River Plate
A World War II Novel

1

Richard G. Hole

World War II

SYNOPSIS

At the outbreak of World War II, England's naval superiority was manifest. The restrictions imposed on Germany by the Treaty of Versailles prevented the creation of a fleet capable of facing the English with chances of success. And although as a result of the naval agreement concluded between the two powers in 1935, Germany gave a great boost to the construction of battle units, when the war broke out on September 1, 1939, Great Britain continued to hold power in all the seas.

The « Admiral Graf Spee », was a pocket battleship that was built by Germany within the narrow margins that had been granted by the victors of the First World War. Its power was inferior to that of most of the ships of the line of other nations, but its construction had been carried out with the care and attention required so that its quality compensated as much as possible for its reduced tonnage and smaller caliber. of her guns, compared to other battleships...

Battle of the River Plate is a story belonging to the World War II collection, a series of war novels set in World War II.

BATTLE OF THE RIVER PLATE

4

FOREWORD

At the outbreak of the second world war, England's naval superiority was manifest. The restrictions imposed on Germany by the Treaty of Versailles prevented the creation of a fleet capable of facing the English with chances of success. And although as a result of the naval agreement concluded between the two powers in 1935, Germany gave a great boost to the construction of battle units, when the war broke out on September 1, 1939, Great Britain continued to hold power in all the seas.

Germany, instructed in the previous conflict, prepared to combat the English power at sea by means of submarine weapons, which was about to produce a frightful collapse in Allied traffic, and the corsair ships that, most of them, dealt hard blows that England evidently; she accused her.

There have been corsairs at all times, and there is no nation that has not used them at some time. They have generally been used by countries that at a given time did not have command of the sea, or else their squads were manifestly inferior in number and power to those of their enemies. Its purpose is to operate in eccentric areas to those dominated by opposing fleets, hunting isolated ships or groups of them without sufficient protection. Their main weapons are surprise, cunning, concealment and speed, and their tactics are constantly changing places and situations in order to avoid being located and pursued.

Germany used corsairs in the two world wars, and used warships or simple merchants armed for that purpose indistinctly. Among the first it is worth mentioning the pocket battleships «Lutzow» and «Admiral Scheer». The Lutzow made several cruises, sinking dozens of merchant ships and finally being able to return to Germany. The second operated in the North and South Atlantic in 1940 and also returned after sinking a British auxiliary cruiser and 152,000 merchant tons, of which 86,000 corresponded to a convoy that was totally annihilated. But the one that most attracted the world's attention was undoubtedly the pocket battleship, twin of the other two, "Admiral Graf Spee", which after having many allied war units in continuous capsizing for several months,

CHAPTER I
THE DEPARTURE

The military port of Wilhelmshaven, an important German naval base, was experiencing very hectic days. Several warships, of various types and tonnage, were anchored in its waters, and in them, in the different docks and warehouses of the base, as well as in the services of the same, an unusual activity could be appreciated. Among all the ships, due to the interest given to it, the fact that any technician would have immediately recognized it as one of the three pocket battleships that the Third Reich navy had at that time was very striking; specifically, the "Admiral Graf Spee".

Evidently the ship was being supplied, outfitted and prepared so that it could be put out to sea shortly, and the screeching of loading cranes mingled with that of the port cars, in constant movement, and the voices of command of the officers.

It was August 23, 1939, and it had been nearly a week since the battleship had been carefully cared for by its entire crew and by a large part of the base's personnel. But at nightfall of that same day the work was finished, the crew of the Graf Spee came aboard, the landmen descended to the docks and the ship was prepared and ready to weigh anchor as soon as it was out. organized.

An hour later, however, as the sun began to sink below the horizon, two men went ashore, and after crossing the harbor esplanade, left the base. They got into a small Mercedes parked by the outer walls, which promptly started off. After crossing several streets of the city, the car approached a wide road lined with tall and corpulent trees through which the first light of twilight filtered. Both men remained silent, one attentive to driving the car and the other lost in thought.

"Do you have a cigarette, Helmut? "asked the driver.

The one called Helmut produced a fancy cigarette case from an inside pocket, which he handed to his companion after opening it. Then he, too, took a cigarette, taking a deep drag.

"I think you're right," he said at last. It's very strange. Never in my years in the Navy have I seen a ship provisioned to such an extent and with such profusion of detail. Not even during maneuvers have we ever carried such a quantity of howitzers and torpedoes, and if we add that nobody, except Langsdorff, knows where we are going, I begin to suspect that there is a cat in all this, a cat with fine teeth and steely nails.

"Helmut" said the other. For many months in Europe a rarefied atmosphere has been breathed. Because of this and other factors, it would not surprise me if before long...

"What?

"Nothing, let's leave it.

Helmut leaned back in his seat, and pushing his cap back as far as it would go, exclaimed:

"I will conclude for you... before long the «Graf Spee» will go hunting in the Atlantic.

His companion looked at him out of the corner of his eye for a moment, immediately going back to concentrating on the maneuvers of the car, which, launched at considerable speed, was devouring kilometer after kilometer.

Minutes later the "Mercedes" left the highway to take a narrow path that wound through a small forest, stopping next to a superb mansion whose walls were climbing a large number of ivy and vines.

"I would like you to do me a favor" said, before leaving the car, the one who was behind the wheel.

"You say, Karl" Helmut said in turn.

"I would appreciate it if you didn't say a single word about what you think in Naty's presence. She believes that our march is one of many, a little longer perhaps, but not important. I wish she would continue to believe so.

"Don't worry, I won't say anything.

Karl pressed the doorbell, and the door opened immediately, through which they both entered.

"Good afternoon, Mrs. Müller" greeted Karl. "Helmut and I have come to say goodbye to you. We're leaving tonight.

"Again? " Mrs. Müller asked, amazed. "But it hasn't been fifteen days since you arrived. It is seen that sailors have to spend their lives in the water. What a profession, my God! Harold did the same; him today he was at home and, suddenly, he left to reappear unexpectedly. Finally, go to the room. I call Naty right away.

Karl and Helmut saw Naty's mother disappear and reappear a little later in the company of her daughter, a girl who was about eighteen years old, markedly dark, with jet-black hair and equally black and brilliant eyes. Her height was more than average, and her body, in general, was not far from perfect.

Both men stood up, and Helmut, twisting his mouth, as if wishing that his words were only picked up by his friend, said:

"I effusively congratulate you. Naty is more beautiful every day. She is a true beauty.

Karl gave his friend a "loving" nudge, forcing him to feel the pit of his stomach insistently, and advanced on the two women.

Naty remained still, silent, with her gaze fixed on Karl, who, once at her side, took her hands in his.

"Naty, we set sail in a few hours. Events have moved forward and Helmut and I have passed our hurdles to be able to come and see you off.

The girl was still silent.

"Anyway" he continued "I hope to be back before a couple of weeks. I know you'll never get used to it, but despite myself, it's not possible to do anything else. You know I'm as sorry as you or maybe more.

"Where are you going? Naty finally asked.

Karl cleared his throat involuntarily and, licking his lips, said:

"We don't know for sure yet, but apparently we're going on maneuvers in the North Atlantic, off the coast of Norway.

"No, Karl "denied her"; You will never be a good liar. I don't know why, but there is something that tells me that this time is not like the previous ones, that it will be a long time before I can see you again.

"For God's sake, Naty" he protested; You talk as if something bad is going to happen to me. Leaving maneuvers does not entail any danger...

Helmut, who until then had remained a mere spectator, interrupted his friend with a forced laugh that made the girl shiver.

"Do you suppose we are going to war? he asked, when the laughter had died on his lips.

Naty's eyes, fixed and deep, forced him to look away.

"I didn't say that much, Helmut," she assured, weighing the words.

Karl wanted the earth to swallow his reckless friend. He had evidently sparked a new idea in her mind.

"Hey, Helmut," he said. Why don't you ask Mrs. Müller to finish showing you her magnificent greenhouse?

"I think it will be for the best," said his friend, scratching his head with the index finger of his right hand and disappearing through the door in the company of Naty's mother.

When Karl and the girl were alone, she raised herself up as high as she could on the tips of her shoes and pressed her face to his, wrapping her shapely arms around his neck.

"Karl, tell me the truth. Where are you going?

He got rid of Naty's hug, and taking a few steps towards the window, he stared through the glass. Helmut was attentive to the explanations that Mrs. Müller was giving him about the plants. His friend's expression of holy resignation made him smile.

"I can't tell you because I don't know. Only Langsdorff knows," he said without turning around. "I have proposed to me, however, to hide from you what I believe, what we all believe; But now you better know I see you suspect something.

"Of course I suspect! "she assured". Moreover, I know. For several days I have been observing you and Helmut, I have captured many of your words that you thought had no meaning for me...

"Fine," Karl cut in. The general belief is that war will soon break out and that the Graf Spee is now putting to sea to be in theater when it does. We may be wrong, but I would be very surprised.

A great silence fell after Karl's words. Only the sound of a clock on the fireplace disturbed the stillness of the environment.

"War! "Naty exclaimed, letting herself fall slowly into a chair. Her cheeks were intensely pale and her eyes were lost at a point I read infinity.

"Yes, the war" he affirmed. It is an assumption, but founded. For several days we have been preparing the ship for a long journey. The medical services have reviewed all the men in the crew one by one, dismissing many due to temporary indispositions that in other circumstances would not have been taken into account. We have shipped a large number of shells and shells of all kinds, including several dozen torpedoes. The holds are full of flour and provisions of all kinds and the tanks are full of water to overflowing, and as if this were not enough, yesterday Langsdorff was locked up in his chamber for several hours talking with three high-ranking commanders of the fleet. All this has only one explanation. Everything has been arranged for a specific purpose and for a specific and serious reason: war.

"I'll pray to God that you're wrong, Karl," Naty said in a barely perceptible voice.

"Do it, yes. Only He can prevent what men do not want to prevent.

The girl got up and went over to Karl and took refuge in his arms as if trying to protect herself from an invisible danger.

"I'm scared" she said. A horrible fear. The idea of losing you forever makes me unbearable. I love you so much, Karl, that if something bad were to happen to you, it would not be possible for me to continue living.

"You shouldn't worry so much, Naty. Even if what we all fear were to happen, it would not be necessary for anything serious to happen to me. Also, knowing that you are waiting for me, I will return; I don't know how or when or in what way, but I'll be back, I promise.

"Thank you, Karl, for giving me encouragement. Women are so stupid!

She raised her eyes to his, and their lips pressed together tightly. Seconds later Karl pulled away abruptly and looked at her watch.

"We have to go, Naty.

"Already?

"Yes. Langsdorff has given us two hours and it's almost over. By the way, he has commissioned me to greet you and your mother on his behalf. He is a great man, and as a sailor there are few who excel him. He has an unusual self-confidence. I am satisfied to be under his command.

At that moment Mrs. Müller and Helmut were returning from the garden. Naty's mother could not hide the satisfaction she had felt at having been able to show someone, extending herself in long pseudo-scientific explanations, her extensive collection of plants and flowers. It seemed to Karl that his friend was totally exhausted and sick.

Both women accompanied the two men to the car. Naty, her eyes filled with tears, hugged Karl for the last time.

"I can never forget that, Karl," she said, sobbing. I couldn't resist repeating it in you.

Karl, showing an intense paleness, almost forced himself away from the girl, and after patiently listening to Mrs. Müller's last recommendations, he opened the car door and got in behind the wheel. Immediately the "Mercedes" started off while Naty waved her hand weakly as a sign of farewell.

"Don't forget that you promised to come back," she shouted, when the car was already fifty meters away from her.

"I won't forget it," Karl assured, sticking his head out the window. Although it would be better never to see you again "he concluded muttering between his teeth.

Naty was already far away and she couldn't hear his last words, but Helmut did hear them, and surprise, disbelief and stupor came together in his eyes.

CHAPTER II
A "POCKET BATTLESHIP"

"What have you said? "He asked.

"No, nothing.

"If I have not misheard, you just said that you would prefer never to return. Can I know why?

"You have misunderstood.

"No, I have not misunderstood," Helmut assured.

"Please change the subject.

"Karl, something strange is happening to you, and don't try to deny me. I've been noticing it for a long time, and your behavior often lacks logic. You have the prettiest girlfriend for miles around and she's smarter than most women to boot, and it happens that in her company you tend to be thoughtful, cold and moody. Do you want to tell me what's wrong with you? Don't you want her? If so, leave her; but then I will tell you that you are completely idiotic.

"I love her with all my soul" assured Karl, so that his friend could not doubt his words.

"So what's wrong with you?

Karl didn't reply. Helmut leaned back in his seat and didn't think it was wise to insist further, arriving, however, at the conclusion that it was more difficult to understand his friend than to square the circle.

Half an hour later the car pulled up in front of the base's main entrance, and the two men climbed aboard the battleship.

In the early hours of the morning, between the screeching of chains and siren blasts, the ship's moorings were released, which, turning slowly to port, approached the mouth of the port, disappearing shortly after swallowed by the fog.

The first light of dawn surprised the battleship sailing, already out of German jurisdictional waters, heading for the Atlantic.

The «Admiral Graf Spee», was, as has already been said, a pocket battleship, which together with the «Lutzow» and «Admiral Scheer», was built by Germany within the narrow margins that had been granted by the victors. from the previous world war. Its power was inferior to that of most of the ships of the line of other nations, but its construction had been carried out with the necessary care and care so that its quality compensated as much as possible for its reduced tonnage and smaller caliber. of her guns, compared to other battleships. She displaced just over ten thousand tons and was armed with four 280-millimeter cannons, distributed in three towers, one forward and two aft. She also had four 150-millimeter cannons, eight 533-millimeter torpedo tubes, various anti-aircraft machine guns and four depth charge launchers. Her speed was less than twenty-five knots, so on this point she was clearly inferior to the battle cruisers, many of them larger and better armed. Her crew was made up of a thousand men, including all the services, and thirty officers, not counting the captain and the second commander.

His command had been entrusted by the General Staff of the fleet to Captain Hans Langsdorff, an excellent sailor, from a family closely linked to the sea and the squadron, and he had already participated in the First World War, as a simple cadet, in no few battles against the English. To command the "Graf Spee» and lead it across the Ocean on the difficult mission assigned to it, Langsdorff was the man to go.

Among the officers were lieutenants Karl Weber and Helmut Berling. The first of them had turned twenty-seven and had been in active service in the Navy for five years, not counting, of course, the years of study and practice spent at the Academy, from which he left with the rank of second lieutenant. His first destination was the cruiser «Staal» from which he was transferred, when ascending some time later, to the battleship «Admiral Graf Spee».

He had no family. His parents died when he was still very young and he had no memory of them. A photograph of his mother, from whom he never parted, and an old watch of his father, constituted the sum of goods that were bequeathed to him by his predecessors. He was taken in by an aunt of his, in whose company he spent most of his life, taking care of him with the affection and care of a true mother and watching over his first steps in life. When, many years later, already at the academy, Karl learned of the good woman's death, he wept for her as if she had been the being who had given him her life.

Helmut Berling was the eldest son of wealthy Munich industrialists, manufacturers of artificial silk, who had not been able to dissuade their son from becoming a sailor. He said that the atmosphere of the factory suffocated him and that he needed the sea breezes to be able to breathe comfortably. The family industry could be carried out perfectly by his father for the time being, and later by his brothers, to whom he graciously ceded the part that might correspond to him in his day. His parents agreed to his wishes convinced that the shock with reality would dissuade him from his purposes. But Helmut had been in the Navy for many years now without showing the slightest sign of regret or weariness.

The two boys had met two years before the Admiral Graf Spee had embarked on her last cruise, when Helmut had been posted to the battleship, and they had fraternized quickly. Langsdorff thought highly of both of them, though on occasion he had had to reprimand them; to Helmut for his inordinate fondness for entertainment, and to Karl for his excessively strange character, which ranged from the most unbridled exaltation to the most absolute despondency, from the most accentuated joy to the most incomprehensible moodiness.

When the first light of dawn appeared on the horizon line on August 24, 1939, the bulk of the German battleship was making its way into the sea, most of its servants oblivious to the fact that they were soon to be the protagonists of one of the most fascinating adventures carried out in the Atlantic by German sailors.

CHAPTER III
THE FIRST PREY

Karl, leaning over the gunwale, gazed intrigued at the silhouette of a merchant ship, the "Altmark", which since leaving Wilhelmshaven had been following insistently in the wake left by the "Graf Spee». Evidently, the «Altmark» accompanied them with a fixed mission, but Karl couldn't find it. The merchantman, although armed, could do little or nothing in case of combat. He was not an oil tanker, whose presence would have been partially justified. What purpose would he have?

On August 28, the battleship reached a point located approximately between the Canary Islands and the Bahamas and approached a ship that at first everyone believed to be Japanese, not only because of particular details of its construction, but also because the merchant ship was called Ussukuma. But the general astonishment grew to the point, when the crew of the «Graf Spee» realized that the merchant ship they were rapidly approaching was not Japanese, but a disguised German tanker, from which the battleship refueled and immediately continued the march.

From that moment Karl had no more doubts about the mission of the German ship. He was fully convinced that war would soon break out; it was a matter of days, maybe weeks, but he couldn't stop coming. Captain Langsdorff, despite the fact that he knew that his men already knew the secret, said nothing. Limiting himself to smiling when the eyes of his officers rested on him questioningly.

The answer was immediate. On the first of September, when almost all of the officers were gathered in the dining room after the noon meal, a man rushed in. Karl recognized him at once as one of the components of the telegraphy and radio services. He carried a paper in his right hand, and after greeting Captain Langsdorff, he handed it over. He unfolded it more slowly than Karl would have liked, though he knew the contents of the report as if he had been reading it dozens of times. Langsdorff, invited by his officers, rose gravely.

"Gentlemen," he said, "at last you are going to know what you have asked yourself so many times and what undoubtedly the majority already assumed. Today, September 1, 1939, Germany is at war with England and France. The Polish border has been crossed at various points in the victorious march on Warsaw. I want you to get your men on deck as soon as possible. I have a few words to say to you."

Most of the officers left the chamber in a hurry to comply with the order. The uproar was indescribable. Karl smiled.

Minutes later the full crew of the battleship was lined up. Langsdorff, from the central bridge command post, addressed his men in these terms:

"Marines! I have just been informed that the Third Reich is at war with England and France. From today our country will begin a hard fight against its enemies, in which all Germans will cooperate to the best of their ability. Powerful are the powers against which we will have to fight, but much greater is our faith and security in victory. For all these reasons, from this precise moment the «Admiral Graf Spee» becomes a corsair ship with the specific mission of hunting down and sinking the largest number of enemy ships and hindering traffic across the Atlantic that could go against the interests of Germany. I have no doubt that because of the greatness of our homeland and because of the prestige of the German Navy, each and every one of us will give the maximum effort of which we are capable, even if it leads us to the sacrifice of our lives.

A deafening scream that erupted in unison from the throats of a thousand men rose from the battleship, spreading across the entire surface of the sea.

From that moment on, the corsair ship would have to navigate cautiously, always alert, staying hidden among the waves of the Ocean, on the lookout for its prey. Always vigilant, always attentive to the lines of the horizon, where the silhouettes of its enemies could appear unexpectedly, the "Graf Spee» had to navigate the waters as a feline scampers through the thick of the jungle, waiting for the propitious victim that served as a target for their cannons.

On the thirteenth of September, two weeks after the beginning of hostilities, the German corsair was stationed in an area over the equator, bearing 200th from Freetown. For fourteen days he unsuccessfully stalked the passage of English ships, and on the twenty-seventh he headed for the American coast, landing in Babia.

On September 30, 140 miles 125th from Pernambuco, the "Graf Spee» made its first kill. At around fourteen o'clock on the indicated day, the German battleship was sailing parallel to the coast of Brazil, when smoke was sighted at a bearing of 320°, which was immediately reported by surveillance services. All eyes turned to the place referred to, and it was verified that, indeed, a column of smoke was rising into the sky over the horizon, twenty-two miles away. The battleship maneuvered, and putting the bow to the located ship, at full speed headed to meet him. Soon it was found that it was an English merchant, approximately five thousand tons and heavily loaded, as indicated by the waterline. The English, who certainly did not expect such an unpleasant encounter, they did not identify the warship sailing towards them until it was too late. Reversing their engines, they tried to maneuver westward, no doubt taking refuge in some neutral port, but the much faster Graf Spee easily cut them off, intercepting their path.

Langsdorff ordered a message to be relayed to him ordering him to stop and surrender himself prisoner, and shortly afterwards the "Clement", as the captured ship was called, lay completely motionless on the waves. Immediately several speedboats full of armed sailors and a few officers, including Karl, reached the sides of the English ship and its occupants climbed aboard.

The captain of the "Clement" danced on deck. The paleness of his countenance contrasted with his intensely dark blue uniform. Most of the crew stood behind him, and some of the men had their lips pursed and their hands clenched. In his eyes the most conflicting emotions could be easily read.

A German lieutenant approached the captain of the merchantman, and waving to him with his hand on his cap, notified him that from that moment he and his men were prisoners of Germany and that they must prepare to be transferred immediately to the "Altmark" as such.

The motorboats set sail again doubly loaded and the "Clement" was left at the mercy of the German battleship.

Karl stayed on board with some sailors, in order to inspect the cargo and seize the ship's documentation. The first consisted of a large quantity of meat, possibly Argentine, and several tons of raw rubber that the Clement must have loaded in some Brazilian port. In the captain's cabin Karl found the documentation he was looking for and the ship's log, as well as other things that he also ordered to be taken in case they could be of use to Langsdorff. They finally abandoned ship and returned to the Graf Spee.

The English ship gently rocked in the waves, outlining its silhouette on the horizon line and awaiting the arrival of the torpedo that would bury it forever in the ocean. A white wake left the German battleship in the direction of the "Clement." A terrible explosion, which spread over the entire surface of the sea, shocked the corsair's first prey, who, mortally wounded, slowly tilted to port to disappear fifteen minutes later under the water.

The English captain had had time to report that he was falling into the clutches of a German corsair battleship, and so Langsdorff deemed it prudent to immediately change the scene. That same day he set sail for the Eastern Atlantic, landing in Loanda (Angola).

CHAPTER IV
IN FULL HUNTING

The sinking of the «Clement» signaled to the General Staff of the English fleet the presence of a German corsair in the waters of the South Atlantic. As most of the combat units that England possessed in that area were light cruisers, for whom the pocket battleship represented a serious danger, an adequate force was immediately prepared that, quickly putting to sea, could hunt down the corsair. before it wreaked more havoc on Allied merchant traffic.

On October 2, 1939, the so-called "K" force commanded by Vice Admiral Wells left "Scapa Flow". This «K» force was composed of the following units: the battle cruiser «Renown», weighing 32,000 tons, with six 381-millimeter guns and twelve 102-millimeter guns. In addition, she had abundant anti-aircraft artillery, four fighter planes and developed twenty-eight and a half knots of speed. The "Ark Royal» aircraft carrier, the most modern in the British fleet, displacing 22,000 tons and armed with sixteen 114-millimeter guns and several anti-aircraft guns. Her speed was up to thirty and a half knots, and her sixty Swordfish and Skua aircraft were a mighty force. Four destroyer escorts completed the formation.

The grouping was perfectly conceived. Vastly more powerful than Admiral Graf Spee and considerably faster than it, Renown could relatively easily overwhelm the pocket battleship as soon as it was brought within range of her guns. The planes of the mighty "Ark Royal» were to sweep the Atlantic until they located the corsair and then lead the "Renown» to him.

Force "K" arrived at Freetown on October 12, when the "Graf Spee» was in Ascension, and after refueling what it needed, it put to sea again in the direction of Saint Helena. For almost a month the British group explored a wide area, limited by the parallel of Saint

Helena, the coast of Liberia and the 0th and 20th meridians of longitude. The aircraft carrier's aircraft did not allow themselves a moment's rest. Two explorations were carried out daily, one at dawn, which ended at ten o'clock, after four hours of flight, and another that began at fourteen o'clock to finish at nightfall. But it was all useless; the German corsair did not appear.

The only positive result achieved by the «K» force during this period was the capture of a German merchant ship. On November 4, a «Swordfish» signaled the presence of a German ship that was heading towards the center of the Atlantic. It was the steamer "Uhenfels", which carried to Germany a rich cargo of hides, nuts, coconut kernels and opium, valued at two hundred and fifty thousand pounds sterling. She was arrested and taken to an English base.

While all this was going on, the "Graf Spee» had continued its raids with singular success.

After sinking the «Clement», and when, fleeing from a possible trap, he was sailing towards Angola, on October 5 he sighted another English merchant ship, the «Newton Beech», weighing 4,650 tons, and, like the one already sunk, heavily loaded. The afternoon was beginning to decline and the first shadows of twilight dyed the Ocean black. As soon as the English steamer identified the German corsair, she turned to port and tried to get away at full speed and get lost in the night. Langsdorff immediately realized the merchantman's intentions and ordered the engines to be forced to catch up with him before it became completely dark. It would have been easy for the "Graf Spee» to sink the "Newton Beech" with her 280-pounders, but Langsdorff did not want to do it, first because he intended to save as much shells as possible, since his stay in the Atlantic was going to be very long and he might need them at the last minute, and secondly because it would have meant the death of the entire crew of the English ship, which he wanted to avoid. Regardless, he was sure the ship would end up in her power and there was no need to force things.

The Newton Beech was sailing at considerable speed, and although the distance between him and the corsair was closing by the minute, when night came between them there were still a dozen miles. Luckily it was a full moon, which greatly facilitated the pursuit of the English ship, which was getting closer and closer. At three o'clock in the morning, Langsdorff warned the merchantman's captain that if he did not stop within fifteen minutes, he would be sunk without further warning by the battleship. The threat took effect, and moments later the German sailors came aboard, completely occupying the ship. At dawn the English crew was transferred to the «Altmark», and after embarking on the «Newton Beech» a crew of prey, they were accompanied by it, landing in Port Gentil (French Equatorial Africa).

Two days later he captured the 4,220-ton Ashlea, loaded with rich skins and dried fish, which, torpedoed, sank after moving the entire crew. The «Ashlea» was the third ship captured by the German corsair and the second sent to the bottom of the sea.

From then on, the "Graf Spee» was placed between French Equatorial Africa and Sierra Leone, a fertile and appropriate area for hunting, and since the "Newton Beech" did not report any use to it at the moment, the ship sank it. october nine next to a small coral reef.

The next day, when he was sailing four hundred miles to the west of Ascension Island, a large English merchant ship, the 8,196-ton Huntsman, suddenly appeared before his eyes. bow to Ascension Island. Langsdorff was not interested in getting too close to that point, as he feared that there might be enemy warships around it; so he called Karl, head of one of the eight-inch turrets.

"Lieutenant Weber" he told him. Stop me immediately to that ship. Keep him from sailing ten more miles.

Shortly after two salvos from the "Graf Spee» forked the merchantman, who immediately proceeded to stop and surrender to the German battleship. Langsdorff arranged for a prize crew to be embarked and to sail with him.

At that time, the commander of the German corsair was completely sure that the English knew of his presence in the Atlantic, and that several warships were already sweeping the sea in search of him. So he decided to change the scene again. Until the twenty-second of October he sailed in a zig-zag two days to the South-West, two days to the South and three days to the North-West.

On the seventeenth he sank the Huntsman, which had been sailing in his company for a little over a week. The merchant ship, hit by two torpedoes, one in the center and the other in the stern, which opened terrible waterways, shook between frightful convulsions and began to sink slowly in a sea of foam and great eddies. A few minutes later she had disappeared from the surface and to the eyes of the German sailors who accompanied her in her agony.

The «Graf Spee» then headed east, and on the twenty-second day hunted down a new merchant ship, the «Trevanion», of 5,299 tons, which was torpedoed and sunk together with its rich cargo of wood.

Two days later Langsdorff summoned his officers. In the meeting chamber sat the captain of the battleship, with the ship's deputy commander to his right. The rest of the officers occupied the chairs placed on both sides of a long table, some remaining standing for lack of sufficient space. Karl conversed with Helmut and Lieutenant Stolff, as the rest of the officers did in groups, waiting for the last stragglers to arrive. Seconds later the chamber door was closed and Langsdorff got up from his seat, then went to a map hanging on one of the walls.

"Gentlemen," he said, "I have called you to give you an exact account of what has been done to date, our situation, possibilities, and the projects I have outlined for the future. I want you to listen to me carefully and ask me, if you wish, the questions you deem appropriate. Today "he went on" it is exactly sixty-one days since we put to sea. In this time we have sunk five enemy merchant ships with a total of approximately thirty thousand tons. It is not much, but it is something considering the circumstances in which we move, without an escort of any kind. We have traveled several thousand miles without luckily encountering English or French warships. But I am convinced, as obviously you are too, that at this moment important formations are looking for us insistently throughout the South Atlantic. If we find any of them on our way, our situation would be extremely difficult. The "Graf Spee» cannot compete with most English cruisers, as they are superior in power or speed. In either case our hunt would begin immediately, and before long we would have a large squad behind us. Our tactic cannot be other than the one we have been following up to now, that is, to strike a quick blow in a certain area to immediately disappear from it and reappear in another as distant as possible. Only in this way will we avoid being located and persecuted closely. My intention is to head for the Indian Ocean, leaving the Atlantic for the time being; if they look for us, which, as I said, I have no doubt, It will be precisely in this Ocean. We will try to sink one or more ships in the Indian Ocean, this will make the English go to that sea, but by then we will be back in the Atlantic".

With a long pointer, Langsdorff had been pointing out on the map the itinerary he intended to follow. The gazes of the officers had been following him with interest.

CHAPTER V
A GLASS OF SHERRY

"There is another point of great importance" continued the captain. It is necessary for me to know the number and importance of the forces that seek us. Our future movements largely depend on it. This point was planned before leaving Germany. Our information had to be supplied to us by a chain of agents who, at different points on the African and American coast, had the specific mission of finding out about the movements of the enemy units and giving us an account of all this by radio. I was mainly expecting to hear from Freetown and Capetown, but apparently something unusual has happened. And since it is vital for us to know where we stand with respect to enemy forces, the information that has failed we will have to provide ourselves. I need two officers to volunteer for a risky mission.

Langsdorff had not finished speaking when all the officers were on their feet.

"Thank you all! said the battleship commander. I expected no less from you. But in view of this, I myself will choose them.

A deep silence fell in the room. All eyes were on Langsdorff, who slowly turned to where Karl was standing.

"Lieutenant Weber," he exclaimed, "are you willing to be one of them?

"Yes, my captain" stated Karl.

Helmut, standing to his right, gave his friend a vicious stomp that forced his leg to visibly shrink.

"My captain," said Karl immediately, "since you have honored me by choosing me precisely, I would like you to allow me to designate the one who will accompany me.

"Okay, Lieutenant," Langsdorff agreed. You name it.

"Lieutenant Berling.

"According. In an hour I'll expect you both in my cabin.

Without another word, Langsdorff left the chamber, followed by his second.

The rest of the officers filed out of the room as well, and Karl and Helmut went up on deck together.

"What will the captain want from us? "asked the second, as if talking to himself.

"And what do I know? Karl exclaimed. In any case, we will know soon.

Lieutenant Stolff approached them.

"It seems to me, boys, that you are going to find yourselves in a big mess soon," he said.

"In a mess? Helmut asked. What kind of mess?

"It's easy to guess," continued Stolff. What does the captain want you for? Obviously so that you provide the missing information. And where are you going to find this information? Well, on land; it is very simple.

"Obviously" confirmed Karl, looking at an indeterminate point on the horizon.

"Hilarious! Helmut opined.

"Yes, very funny," said Stolff.

"But in what place? Helmut asked again.

"I think you want to know everything ahead of time," Karl said. But if it helps you, I'll tell you that since this morning we've been sailing towards Capetown.

"This would be walking into the lion's den," Stolff said, his eyes widening, "or at least into his lair.

There was a deep silence. Karl smoked a cigarette and his eyes remained fixed on the horizon. Helmut amused himself throwing paper balls into the sea and Stolff blankly watched his friend in his useless operation.

"Karl," Stolff said suddenly, "do you want me to go instead?

Karl turned, quick as lightning.

"No way! "He said". Also, what for?

"Yes, Karl," said Helmut in turn. Hans is right. You have more interest than us in returning to Germany one day. Let him come with me.

"I beg you not to insist on such an absurdity," asked Karl.

"As you like," said Helmut. But I would really appreciate it if you could answer a question for me before starting this adventure, from which we may not return.

"What question?

"On the day of our departure from Wilhelmshaven, you said something very strange, on which I have often been pondering ever since. Is it true that you would rather never return to Germany? Why? What happens between you and Naty?

Karl tossed the cigarette overboard, and turning slowly, his back was to the sea.

"That" he said "is three questions, not one. I'll wait for you in half an hour in the captain's cabin. Plunging his hands into his pockets, he walked off in the direction of the central bridge, leaving Helmut completely bewildered. Stolff brought him back to reality with a pat on the shoulder.

"Hey, Helmut," said the lieutenant, "it's natural to be intrigued by Karl's behavior and to want to know what's wrong with him if you've noticed something strange. But it is better that you do not ask him any more questions about this particular. He will thank you.

"Okay, Hans," Helmut agreed. But you will agree with me that Karl's behavior would intrigue anyone. On the other hand, I am his best friend and he has never kept anything from me, why should he now?

"Look, boy," continued Stolff. We all have things in life that we prefer to hide, even from our best comrades. You have known Karl for barely two years, but I was with him at the Academy first and at the

"Staal" later. Together we were transferred to the "Graf Spee» and I know his life and his problems as if it were me. Trust me, don't ask him any more questions, you'll find out one day.

"Then, do you know?

"Yes, I know. But not because he told me about it, but because I lived it too.

Helmut stared at his friend, his eyes questioning.

"No. I won't tell you anything," continued Stolff. I can't tell you, it's a secret that doesn't belong to me. It happened more than three years ago and I have never said a word to anyone. Don't expect me to do it now.

"You say that the cause of Karl's inexplicable behavior took place more than three years ago, so presumably it would be something serious. This is the only way to justify maintaining an annoying and unpleasant attitude for so long. Don't you think?

"You have mistaken the profession," said Stolff, smiling. You should have been a diplomat. Yes, you are right. It was something very serious, or at least "the lieutenant continued looking absently at the sky" it seems so.

"Does Naty have something to do with all this?

"End of broadcast," Stolff said, lighting a cigarette. You better go see the captain. It must be waiting for you.

Giving a resigned sigh, Helmut walked away visibly sulky. Karl was already waiting for him outside Langsdorff's cabin door. After knocking and having been granted permission to enter, both men entered the room. Langsdorff was engrossed in studying a map of the West African coast spread out on a table. Beside him, the second commander of the battleship was writing down in a small pocket notebook a long series of names, numbers and signs. They were invited to sit down, which they gladly did in small but comfortable leather upholstered chairs. Langsdorff placed goblets in front of them, which he then filled to the brim with gold-colored liquid.

"Spanish sherry! "She said smiling." There is nothing better.

The four men joined their glasses in a toast to the distant homeland, and Helmut, after taking a long drink, promised himself to visit Spain carefully as soon as possible.

CHAPTER VI
CAPETOWN ROAD

"As I told you an hour ago "Langsdorff began", you will have to carry out a dangerous and important mission. I have chosen you, Lieutenant Weber, for two reasons: first, because you are fluent in English, and second, because I consider you fully capable of carrying out the task at hand. His choice was also fortunate.

Helmut swelled in his chair as the captain's eyes rested on him.

"The «Graf Spee»" continued the commander of the ship "operates completely alone in a sea infested with enemies. But what worries me the most is the lack of knowledge we have of the number, quality and situation of it. The reports that we expected to receive, for some unknown reason, have not arrived. Your mission is to go in search of such information. Precisely. "Langsdorff here emphasized his words" to the English naval base in Capetown.

Helmut, despite the fact that, like Karl and Stolff, he already guessed their destination, could not prevent the hairs on his head from standing on end. Entering a British naval base in time of war seemed to him to be a highly inadvisable adventure. Karl, for his part, showed no emotion.

"In the city of Capetown, and exactly at this address," continued the captain, handing Karl a neatly folded piece of paper, "lives a man whom the English know as Tony Andreotti and assume to be Italian. He is actually Austrian and his real last name is Vessel. Some years ago he settled in Capetown, developing a prosperous business tanning fine skins and establishing great friendships, through his splendor and generosity, with a number of the most outstanding English and European officers. His real job is to provide Germany with invaluable information, as an agent of the Third Reich, on African naval bases and the movement of allied squadrons. He had to provide us with the necessary data to be able to navigate relatively safely, but, as I said, something unexpected seems to have happened.

Helmut listened intently to Langsdorff's explanations, his eyes widening and futilely trying to moisten his dry throat. He gulped down the rest of the contents of his glass, cursing under his breath that he wasn't much older.

"Now is the time for you to appear on the scene. Tonight we will reach a point near the African coast, about sixty miles north of Capetown. In a motorboat and in the company of two sailors, whose choice I leave to your good judgment, they will go to land. Shortly before reaching it they will stop, and in a rubber boat the two of you must reach the coast as close as possible to Capetown, after memorizing the exact location of the speedboat in order to return to it. They will then go to the city and look for the tanner Tony Andreotti, from whom they will obtain reports. In the possible case that something has happened to our agent, they will try by all means to find out if there are war units anchored in the base, their type and number and if possible the probable arrival of other ships. If, unfortunately, you were arrested, on the ground you would have to look for the best way out, but, although it goes without saying, for no reason, whatever it may be, you will have to reveal the presence of the "Graf Spee» in these waters. Also instruct the men who accompany you, so that in the case of being in danger, of being captured while waiting, they go into the sea if the threat comes from land, or so that they disappear into the jungle if they fear being arrested from behind. the sea. As soon as they have left the ship tonight, we will put to sea again, returning in four days to this same point to pick them up. In the event that you have not arrived, we will return the following night, and if you have not returned either, we will have no other choice but to disappear forever.

Langsdorff got to his feet and Karl and Helmut followed suit.

"Get your things ready and be ready in three hours. Dress in civilian clothes, not very new, and refrain from carrying any documentation or objects that could give you away.

Outside the captain's cabin, Helmut patted his friend on the back.

"You must be happy, right? "I ask". It seems to me that your wishes not to return to Germany will be granted.

Karl took it upon himself to choose the two men who were to accompany them. Two young and strong boys, since the vicissitudes that, if things went wrong, could happen, required such conditions. At twenty-three hours, well after dark, the battleship came to a complete stop. A motorboat equipped with everything necessary was launched and the two sailors chosen by Karl went down to it, Langsdorff warmly shaking hands with both officers and giving them the last recommendations.

"Take this with you, you may need it, especially Lieutenant Berling. "Helmut took from the captain a bottle carefully wrapped in cardboard paper.

"Sherry? "He asked.

"Sherry" affirmed the captain.

"Thanks sir.

Langsdorff then handed Karl a blue envelope.

"Once you have located Tony Andreotti," he said, "you will give him this envelope. This will dispel all misgivings from him and make you put yourself at his disposal. Good luck!

Karl and Helmut quickly descended into the speedboat, ready to set sail. Stolff, leaning over the rail, waved them off.

"Say hello to the prettiest girl in Capetown for me," he yelled as his friends began to walk away from the boat.

"Don't worry," assured Helmut. We will do it.

The boat was lost in the shadows and the hum of its engine was becoming weaker by the moment, until it died out completely.

All night they sailed in a straight line towards the coast, and when a slight bluish tint in the sky told them that the rising of the sun was near, they headed south towards the English base.

"Watch out! Karl suddenly shouted, pointing to a point in the distance. A ship sails in that direction.

All eyes turned to the indicated place. A column of black smoke rose into the sky, some ten miles from where they stood.

"Without a doubt it is an English ship. She is heading north, leading to the assumption that she is from Capetown. It is convenient to stop, the trail we left behind could give us away.

The speedboat stopped and lay rocking on the waves. The four men, stretched out inside it, eagerly followed the progress of the steamer, which gradually moved away, heading north, until it was lost in the sea.

"If they follow this course," said Karl, "they will be in the hands of the Graf Spee before long." Capetown can't be far enough, eight miles or so. I think we'd better head for land.

The boat was thrown into the water and both officers moved into it after giving the last instructions to the sailors.

"You must not let yourselves be caught by the English. I have already told you how you have to react in case you see yourself in danger. Tonight try to get a little closer to the ground and above all protect yourself from the sun; Sunstroke could be fatal.

"And don't finish all the sherry," he added. Helmut. "Leave me something for when I get back.

Both friends rowed for a long time, finally reaching land. From the motorboat the sailors followed them with their eyes until they disappeared among the thick vegetation of the coast.

CHAPTER VII
IN THE HEART OF THE JUNGLE

"It's a nice ballot they've handed us," said Helmut, pausing for a moment and wiping the sweat from his brow. To cross several miles of virgin jungle infested with vermin of all kinds, to end up resting among the English in one of their best defended naval bases, would restore lost health to anyone.

"Come on man! Karl encouraged him. We can't waste time. Tonight we have to reach the gates of Capetown to enter the city taking advantage of the darkness.

They resumed their march, making their way through the thick vegetation. Lianas and twisted tree trunks made their progress extremely difficult. Sometimes they sank up to their knees in thick layers of mud and muck that the recent rains had formed, only to walk on sharp, angular stones that tortured their feet despite their shoes.

They arrived at the banks of a fairly mighty river, over whose waters spread the thick branches of the trees that grew on its banks. An army of monkeys of all sizes fled in his path, while a deafening racket thundered through space.

"We'll have to swim across it," Karl opined. We don't have the time or the means to build a raft.

"In agreement. But it wouldn't do me any good to end up serving some crocodile as an appetizer.

"These little animals only appear in novels and in movies," assured Karl. Do not worry.

They quickly undressed, and, making a bundle of their clothes, fastened them over their heads with the belts. They then dove into the water.

"After all, a bath will do us good," Helmut opined.

They were a little over halfway across the river when Karl gave a warning cry.

"Run Helmut! Swim fast, with all your might.

"What's going on? "Asked his friend.

"Ask no questions and do as I tell you.

A little later they reached the opposite bank, panting and half exhausted. Helmut shrugged off the weight of his clothes and took a deep breath.

"Do you want to tell me what happened to you? "She asked.

"Turn around and you will see.

Barely ten meters away, an enormous crocodile opened its elongated jaws, looking at them greedily.

"Hilarious! Helmut said. Apparently the authors of those novels that you referred to a moment ago come to these places to be inspired. What a coincidence!

After drying off and dressing, they continued on their way. Their arms and legs were covered in blood. The thorns of the bushes dug into their flesh without hardly noticing it and numerous swarms of mosquitoes greedily fed on their wounds. Suddenly Helmut leapt to the envy of any Olympic champion, and quick as a flash drew his pistol from his holster.

"Still! Karl yelled at him. Don't shoot, you might draw attention.

"Then what do I do? Helmut asked, his eyes bulging.

"But what happens? I don't see anything abnormal.

"Not, huh? Deign to turn your head to the right and you will find out.

So Karl did. Very close to them a huge snake slithered through the leaves.

"It doesn't matter," assured Karl. It is a boa, a very unhappy animal.

"An unhappy animal, you say? Well, it doesn't seem like it. Anyway, for whatever it may be, you'd better get the hell out of this place. I'll be back next year to build myself a little house with a garden.

It was dark when they saw the first lights of Capetown. The vegetation extended uninterrupted until very close to the city, so it was relatively easy for them to approach the first houses without being seen.

"From this moment on," Karl said, "it is best to walk as if nothing had happened. Put your hands in your pockets and try to sing a happy song. We must adopt a carefree air.

Shortly after, both friends were walking down a moderately lit street where some dark-skinned Indians were walking. From time to time a white man, with a wide-brimmed hat and pale dresses, crossed his path. Suddenly Karl's blood ran cold in his veins. Helmut, with a cigarette at the corner of his mouth, was whistling a song just as he had been advised. The song was nice, but it was called "Rose Marie" and it was German. Two seconds later Helmut's cigarette had fallen from his lips and he was feeling the pit of his stomach sourly.

On the paper that Langsdorff had given them, in addition to writing down the name of the street where Tony Andreotti lived, a map had been drawn so that it would be possible for them to find his address without having to ask anyone, and in this way after After an hour and a half of running around the city, they stopped in front of a house painted white with some red brick trim.

"Here it is," said Karl. It's ten p.m. Presumably our friend is home by now.

But he was wrong. After knocking by means of an old bell attached to the top of the door, the door was slowly opened and a black man, who must have been approximating six feet in height, appeared in the doorway.

"Mr. Andreotti, are you at home? Karl asked.

"No, gentlemen" the black man expressed himself in a complicated jargon mixture of English and some indigenous dialect, but he made himself understood. The gentleman has gone out, like every night, for a walk.

"And where could we find it?

The black man hesitated. It occurred to Karl that Andreotti had possibly instructed him not to give anyone information about his movements.

"We are friends of yours," continued Karl. We have just arrived from the interior and need to see him on a matter of great interest to him.

"The gentlemen can return in an hour if they wish. I don't know where he has gone. "The servant closed the door, leaving both officers in the street.

"Dammit! He exclaimed indignantly, Helmut. So, what can we do now?

"Well, exactly what the black man said. We'll turn around and be back in a bit.

They continued walking down the same street, and soon they found themselves in a wide square from which there was a wide view of the moonlit sea.

"Beautiful panorama! Helmut sighed. No one would say that the "Graf Spee» hides near here.

"Please shut up and don't commit any more imprudence. Let's go into that bar... or whatever.

Through the door of a building located in the same square, the sounds of an amusing song were filtered, mixed with the voices of men and the noise of bottles and glasses colliding.

They entered the premises. An atmosphere thickened by tobacco smoke and the perspiration of many bodies almost made Helmut back, but seeing that Karl was already inside, he followed. They approached a long and unclean wooden counter, ordered two cognacs and, after finishing them, turned to face the center of the place, where two indigenous women dancers were dancing to the beat of a monotonous and catchy little music. Karl ran his eyes over the farthest corners. At a table across the room several naval officers sat drinking the contents of a bottle of whiskey nonstop, laughing and chatting animatedly. The entrance of both friends had attracted attention and several eyes were fixed on them. They tried their best to behave naturally, soon managing to stop being the target of all eyes. Only one of the officers sitting in front of the liquor bottle kept scrutinizing them carefully, testing Helmut's nerves.

The indigenous women finished their dance amidst a round of applause with which the public rewarded their work. Karl also applauded without great enthusiasm, while Helmut ordered their empty cups to be refilled. The room was illuminated more intensely and through one of the doors that gave access to the rear part of the premises a young woman dressed in a completely white "evening" dress appeared.

"This is better now," Helmut opined, after letting out a high-pitched whistle that he couldn't suppress.

The girl, who was then singing the first bars of a popular French song, could not have been more than twenty-five years old. She was extremely slender, and her blond hair contrasted with the tan color of her complexion. She was also remarkably pretty, and the nuances of her voice pleased both friends, especially Helmut, who was looking at her in fascination.

"Until we're back on board," said Karl, "forget that you're German and always express yourself in English, even when you're alone. If you're not more careful, we're going to find ourselves in big trouble.

Without stopping singing, the girl approached Karl and Helmut with a charming smile that made Helmut shiver. Karl, for his part, was more attentive to the English officer who did not take his eyes off them, than to the sympathies of the young woman. She came up to the counter, and stopping in front of Karl she lovingly took him by the arm.

"Good! Helmut said. "And I can be struck by lightning, right?

It seemed as if the pretty girl sang exclusively for Karl, not caring much about the presence of other people in the room. Her voice became softer, more caressing.

*"Breeze that comes down from the distant mountains,
Quench in my chest with your icy breath, The volcano that
devours me».*

"Wow! Helmut exclaimed, perplexed.

*"At last you left the seas
To contemplate you in the deep blue of my eyes.*

Helmut sweated ink. What would she have meant by "at last you
left the seas"? Would she know something?

Karl was now looking at the girl, who, leaning on his arm, did not
take her eyes off his. She finally finished the song and left followed by
a standing ovation. The German lieutenant swallowed the contents of
his cup in one go, and was about to leave the premises followed by his
friend, when he saw that the English officer, who had been watching
them so insistently, was approaching them.

CHAPTER VIII
JENNY

"Good evening, gentlemen," the officer greeted. "Let me introduce myself. His Majesty's Navy Lieutenant Charles Hall.

Karl returned a slight nod.

"My name" he said "is Morris, Arthur Morris, hunter. This gentleman is my partner, John Sheffield.

Karl and Helmut shook hands with the Englishman.

"My colleagues and I" he continued "we have realized that you are very alone. We would be honored if you would deign to sit at our table. We are celebrating great news, of great importance to us.

"Oh yeah? Helmut said, bored.

"Indeed, gentlemen. Barely a couple of hours ago we learned that our aircraft carrier «Ark Royal», which was believed to be lost, was not sunk by German aviation, as was originally said, but on the contrary it is safe and sound sailing through the Atlantic. Understand, gentlemen, that, having all of us good friends on such a ship, the news has made us very happy. Do you accept our invitation?

"With great pleasure! Karl agreed, starting to walk towards the table occupied by the English officers. There were four of them, including Lieutenant Jenkins, and they all rose to their feet as Karl and Helmut arrived. After the required introductions, they once again occupied their corresponding seats.

"That is to say," said one of them, filling the glasses of the two Germans, "that you are hunters. What benefit does such a risky profession bring them?

"Furs," Karl answered quickly. Fine skins, mainly leopard, panther and snake. They are quoted at a good price.

"Who buys them?

"Until now, the city of Bloemfontein was our main market. But nowadays we have had to do without it, due to the hostile attitude of certain tribes. The natives oppose our hunts, despite the fact that they are carried out within the strictest legality, and in order to avoid unpleasant incidents, we have chosen to try to sell our last game in Capetown.

"Will they find someone to buy them here?

"We hope so, even though we don't know anyone; but as our merchandise is coveted and the price is reasonable, we will certainly find someone who is interested in them.

"Where are the skins now?

Karl was starting to get annoyed and so many questions. But, bite the bullet, he continued to lie to him.

"A few miles inland. They are kept by our servants, awaiting orders to bring them to the city.

"My wife has asked me several times to send her a whole snake skin to make I don't know what," Lieutenant Jenkins said. Do you have stock?

"Indeed, many and good. My partner will choose it for you, he is a specialist in this kind of reptiles "said Karl, smiling.

"Very grateful," exclaimed the lieutenant. And tell me, Mr. Sheffield, how do you hunt such dangerous animals?

"Dangerous? Helmut asked, forcedly laughing. But snakes are very unhappy creatures, aren't they, Arthur? I don't always use the same method; This depends on the class in question, size and season of the year. I generally use special traps, but on more than one occasion I have been forced to finish off one that was too rebellious by smashing its skull with a stone.

Karl almost burst out laughing. Helmut was evidently frightened by his own words, and he imagined with horror what an unsuccessful role he would play if he were forced to demonstrate his heroics.

The English officers regarded both friends with admiration and respect, except for Lieutenant Jenkins, whose eyes shone with a strange light.

"Do you have a cigarette, Mr. Morris? "He said suddenly." I have run out.

"I'm sorry, Lieutenant," Karl lamented. It's been a while since I finished them too.

Helmut reached into his pocket for his cigarette case, but a superb kick from Karl stopped him. An English officer handed out cigarettes to everyone, and the conversation carried on animatedly.

"Hello Jenny! "Lieutenant Jenkins said after a while, getting up. Karl turned his head. Behind him was the girl who moments before had chosen him as the recipient of her song. She had exchanged her flowing white dress for a yellow street dress, in which she was truly beautiful. They all stood up.

"Allow me to introduce these gentlemen," said Jenkins, "Messrs. Morris and Sheffield, both hunters. Miss Jenny Saife.

Both young men bowed respectfully. She returned them with a pleasant smile.

"I thought you were initially French," said Karl, inviting her to sit down, "you have a perfect command of Moliere's language.

"I have something French, indeed. I was born in Denmark, but have lived most of my life in France and England, and have been in Capetown for about a year. You, guys, are new in town, right?

"The gentlemen" Jenkins interrupted "are hunters, as I have already told you. They have just arrived from the interior with a shipment of furs that they intend to trade in the city.

"Furs? Do you already have a buyer? Jenny asked.

"No lady; We don't know anyone here, but we'll find him.

"In that case," continued the girl, "perhaps I can help you.

"You?

"Yes. I know the main tanner and dealer in furs in these parts. I mean Tony" said the young woman, addressing Lieutenant Jenkins.

"Well, it's true!" he exclaimed. "How could it not have occurred to me before?

Helmut's blood ran cold. No doubt they were referring to the man they were looking for, the German agent.

"If I'm not going to bother you, I'd appreciate it if you could put me in touch with him," Karl asked, unperturbed.

"I will do it very gladly" assured Jenny. "It so happens that he lives near here; I myself will accompany you.

The orchestra began the first bars of "Perfidia", the famous Spanish dance piece that was all the rage at the time throughout Europe. It seemed to Karl that there was something perfidious in everyone's behavior. In Jenkins, in Jenny and in himself.

"Do you invite me to dance? "asked the girl, turning to Karl.

Karl left his seat, and in the company of Jenny made his way to the dance floor. He wrapped his right arm around her waist and blended in with the other couples.

"Have you been hunting for a long time? Jenny asked suddenly.

"I think I've done it my whole life. Africa has no secrets for me.

"It's weird," she continued. You dance very well for having lived a large part of your life among beasts.

"It is simple intuition. I have a remarkable ear for music and it is not difficult for me to follow the rhythm of an uncomplicated melody.

They both fell silent. Jenny kept her eyes on Karl's face, and Karl kept looking at Helmut, deep in animated conversation with the English officers.

"Are you English?" the girl asked.

"Yes, even though, as I have already told you, I have lived almost always in Africa.

"Your country is at war. Is he not going to do anything for her?

Karl got a lump in his throat.

"I would gladly do for my country what it asked of me, even if it was my own life.

Jenny fixed her blue eyes on his, as if trying to read his thoughts. Karl felt that the girl's right hand exerted a slight pressure on her fingers and that her body pressed against his, closing the distance between them.

"Would you even dare to penetrate an enemy naval base to procure information? "She asked, underlining her words.

Karl shuddered. For a moment impenetrable darkness clouded his eyes and he felt his legs go weak.

"Yes, even this would do," he concluded at last.

The orchestra finished the last bars and they both returned to the table. The English officers were attentive to the explanations and details that Helmut came up with about the hunt for snakes, undoubtedly inspired by an excess of whiskey.

"It's getting late," Jenny said, not sitting down. "If you wish, I will accompany you to Tony's house.

"I think it will be for the best," Karl said.

Both friends said goodbye to the English officers, and in the company of the girl were about to leave the room when Lieutenant Jenkins yelled at them:

"Will you stay long in the city?

"Possibly a few days," Karl replied. "Until we sell all of our skins.

"That being the case, tomorrow we will wait for you here again. Mr. Sheffield has to finish telling us how snakes are hunted.

"We will not miss" added Helmut. I'll even explain to you how his bites should be healed.

Karl and Helmut, accompanied by Jenny, went out into the street.

CHAPTER IX
TONY

The bell in the tanner's house chimed merrily. Seeing that no one answered the call, Helmut insisted again. Presently the door swung ajar, the black face of the servant appearing in the gap, who, after laying his eyes carefully on Jenny, ended by letting them in.

"The gentleman has just arrived," he said. "I have already announced his previous visit and he begs you to please come into the room.

Karl cursed his improvidence a thousand times. He looked sideways at Jenny and it seemed to him that the girl smiled discreetly.

The black invited them to accommodate themselves in two mesh chairs, later disappearing behind some hemp curtains. A few minutes passed, during which both friends and Jenny kept a deep silence. A little later the curtains were parted again, and a man of about forty-five, tall and lean, appeared on the scene. His eyes, bright and moving, resembled those of a fox, and his gait reminded Karl of the big cats in the Hamburg park.

"What a nice surprise, Jenny! "He said, bending as much as he could before the girl and kissing her hand." To what do I owe such an unexpected visit?

Karl and Helmut had risen to their feet, and the young woman was sharing her gaze with the three men.

"By chance" she said "I have met these gentlemen today. They have a sizeable shipment of furs and I thought you might be interested. They are Messrs. Morris and Sheffield, hunters. "Then turning to Karl and Helmut, she added:" This is Mr. Andreotti.

He stepped forward just enough to shake hands with both friends. "Wow, wow! he exclaimed. Skins, huh? What kind of skins?

"Mostly good," answered Karl. "Leopard and snake. But we have some black fox, lion and ox.

"Where are they?

"Ten miles from here, as soon as we have a market we will bring them.

"I think my presence is of no use," Jenny said, getting up. "I'll wait until they've finished walking in the garden" and without waiting any longer, she left the room.

"Have you hunted much?" Andreotti asked, taking a chair across from his visitors.

"So-so," Karl replied.

"Large pieces?

"Some exceeded six thousand tons.

"How? Do you intend to laugh at me?" Andreotti asked with an impenetrable expression.

"By no means," denied Karl. The "Huntsman" reached eight thousand kilos and the "Clement" and the "Trevanion" exceeded five thousand.

"I never heard such names. Are these rare pieces?

"Rare, yes; but not terrestrial, but maritime. Now they are shapeless junk heap at the bottom of the ocean; but a few days ago they sailed the seas under the English flag.

Andreotti got up and slowly went to a small cabinet from which he took out a bottle of cognac and three glasses. He placed two of these on a table in front of Karl and Helmut and filled them up next.

"What do you want from me? "He asked, staring at the liquor falling into the glasses.

Karl held out his hand, a blue envelope protruding from his fingers.

"This is for you," he said. Read it and you will know what we want.

Andreotti tore open the envelope, extracting from it an equally blue piece of paper. He unfolded it slowly and immersed himself in reading its contents. Helmut felt his forehead bathed in cold sweat.

Could they really trust this man? As Langsdorff told them, he was Austrian and had lived among the English for many years. What would be his true position? Wouldn't he lead them into a trap? Why hadn't he informed the Graf Spee?

Tony Andreotti finished the reading, folded the paper and set it on fire with a match. He then closed the doors and drew the hemp curtains.

"You are not without courage," he said, "but you have walked into the lion's den. I have not been able to inform Captain Langsdorff because it has been totally impossible for me to do so. The English have been suspicious of me for a long time, although they know how to hide it very well; You have to admit they're not stupid. I have a station in my fur-drying shed outside the city, but I can't go near it, as the British have located it and are constantly guarding it for someone to use it. I have tried every conceivable means of communicating with you, but all have failed.

"Something like that we assumed," said Karl.

"How did you get here?

"Using a motorboat that we have hidden about eight miles to the north.

"How have you met Jenny?

"She was introduced to us by some English officers a while ago; in a hall that is in a square near here and whose name I do not remember.

"Officers you say? Do you know their names?

"I only remember one. Lieutenant Jenkins.

"Jenkins!" Andreotti exclaimed. "Precisely Jenkins! He is in charge of watching over me day and night. At this time he will be hanging around the house waiting to see or hear something.

"They seemed very friendly," said Helmut. "I don't think they suspect us.

"Not, huh? Do not trust appearances. What objects are they carrying?

"Almost nothing," answered Helmut. The handkerchief, a few pounds sterling and cigarettes.

"What kind of cigarettes?

"Kub.

"Give them to me right away" ordered Andreotti, taking their corresponding stocks from both of their hands. "Has it ever occurred to you that the Englishmen would be very surprised if two hunters from the interior smoked German cigarettes?

Helmut then understood why his friend had given him that superb kick an hour earlier.

"This is all very well," said Karl. "But what interests us most is that you provide us with the information that we have come for so that we can leave immediately.

"Everything will go. Tell me first where the «Graf Spee» is.

Karl hesitated for a moment.

"Near here" he said at last.

"Exactly where?

"For the moment it will be enough for him to know that he walks in these waters," answered Karl.

"I can see that they distrust me. I can't blame him. Now listen to me carefully. I will march with you as soon as possible. If he was still here, he would soon be arrested. We will probably have difficulties and perhaps some will not be able to reach the «Graf Spee». That is why it is necessary that the three of us know what Captain Langsdorff is interested in so that we can inform him on his account regardless of the fate of the other two. Right now, "he continued," a powerful English naval formation is sailing full steam ahead here. It is made up of the heavy cruiser "Renown» and the aircraft carrier "Ark Royal", with fifty-eight aircraft on board, as well as four destroyers. It is necessary that the "Graf Spee» leave these waters immediately and look for a new area of operations, otherwise she would be sunk without remedy.

"Langsdorff had thought of sailing to the Indian Ocean," Karl said.

"Excellent idea!" Andreotti approved. "In said sea the English do not have a considerable force, at most some destroyer that does not imply serious danger for the «Graf Spee». Further south, on the American coast, England has another naval formation in constant movement. It is made up of the cruisers "Cumberland», "Exeter», "Ajax» and "Achilles», commanded by Commodore Harwood. An encounter with our battleship might put her in serious trouble, but never such as she would be if she were forced to meet Renown in unequal combat.

At that moment someone knocked on a door. Andreotti motioned for Helmut to open it, and Helmut did so. Jenny entered the room.

"I think the price is somewhat exaggerated," said the German agent, turning to Karl and pretending he hadn't noticed the girl's presence.

"There are prices," she said, "that are never exaggerated.

CHAPTER X
A WOMAN LIKE MANY

Andreotti turned slowly to Jenny, who was busy gathering the stems of a small bouquet of various flowers, cut in the garden of the house.

"You think so? "he asked.

"Naturally," she answered, smiling. "I am sure that what these gentlemen offer you is more than worth what they ask for.

"It must be true if you say so," Tony answered. Turning then to Karl, he continued: "If the skins are of the quality that you have assured me, I am willing to keep the whole batch if you give me a ten percent discount on the price initially negotiated.

"Agreed," Karl said, getting up. "I will immediately order my porters to bring the cargo to Capetown. Tomorrow, or at the latest the day after tomorrow, they will be here.

"Do you already have accommodation?" Andreotti asked.

"No. We have only arrived five hours ago and we have not been able to deal with it.

"In that case I would be most honored if you would accept my modest hospitality. My house is simple and lacks luxuries, but you will feel better in it than in any hotel in the city, where the most basic cleanliness is conspicuous by its absence.

"But. "Karl started a small protest" we are afraid of causing inconvenience.

"No way! "said the German agent." His company will be very pleasant to me. By the way, have you guys had dinner? No? I immediately order them to prepare something.

Andreotti walked to one end of the room, sounding a small gong on a small table. Barely a minute passed, the hemp curtains parted, and the hulking figure of the black man appeared.

"Togo" said his master, "order your wife to prepare a good dinner for... You, have you eaten yet, Jenny? "He asked the girl." Yes?... for two people.

Togo quickly disappeared. Helmut found the prospect of a good meal delicious. They hadn't had a bite to eat for long before they left the motorboat, and he felt as if his stomach had been "ironed" by a steamroller.

"I have to go now," Jenny said, making a move to get up. "My mission is over.

"In no way! Andreotti protested. "Unless you have some inescapable commitment.

"No, I have no commitment" assured the girl. "But these gentlemen will be tired and will want to retire soon.

"No, miss," Helmut denied. "We are used to sleeping little. A few hours are enough for us to fully recover. Also, with this oppressive heat, we could hardly fall asleep.

"You better stay" Andreotti opined. "These gentlemen are evidently unaccustomed to being in the company of such pretty girls.

"Thank you, Tony," she thanked. "You're very gallant.

Jenny sat down again. Karl was now looking at the girl with special interest, and he had to admit that she was indeed very pretty. He wondered to himself what mystery Jenny's life held and what her true existence had been. Currently she was dancing at a Capetown nightspot; but what would she have done in the past? What long chain of hardships and sufferings would she have had to endure perhaps?

The girl turned her head slightly and her eyes met his. For a long time they stared at each other in silence. The sweetness of Jenny's features made a deep impression on Karl. In her blue eyes, which began to fascinate the German lieutenant, reflected a calm and serenity that deeply impressed him, while in her mouth, perfectly outlined, a slight hint of bitterness could be guessed.

Andreotti deliberately cleared his throat and Karl came back to reality. Helmut amused himself preparing a "cocktail", mixing for this purpose, in an appropriate container, part of the content of all the bottles that he found inside the bar cabinet. The mixture took on an indefinite blackish color, but the taste was not unpleasant.

Togo reappeared again, announcing that dinner was served, and the master of the house led both friends and Jenny into the dining room. The food was succulent and all of it passed in animated talk. Subjects as disparate as war, wild beast hunts, in whose technique Helmut ended up consecrating himself as a true notability, literature and music were touched upon. Karl noticed right away that Jenny had an unusual culture, which surprised him, given the environment in which she lived. After dessert, the girl expressed her desire to leave, and Karl gladly offered to accompany her.

"You are a strange woman," he said, when both were already in the street.

"Why?

"You have a remarkable culture. You knows most of the English, German and Spanish classics and is also involved in modern literature. This, and forgive me, is not in line with... your way of making a living.

Karl immediately regretted having spoken so abruptly. Jenny's face reflected deep sadness. They walked for a long time in silence, crossing several streets, most of them dimly lit.

"Sometimes" said the girl "we are not allowed, out of imperative necessity, to choose the kind of life we would have wanted. I don't dance in a nightclub for pleasure, Mr. Morris, but because, at the moment, I need it in order to go on living.

"I beg your pardon, Jenny," Karl humbly requested. "I didn't mean to upset her. Surely I did not know how to express what I was trying to say. I mean that, having a more than careful education, it would not be difficult for you to find another kind of work more suitable to you.

"I have searched for it repeatedly, but I have been unable to find it.

"Why don't you tell me about your life, Jenny?" Karl asked.

"Are you really interested? she asked, staring at him.

"Yes, I am very interested.

"I'll give you a quick summary. I was born, as I told you before, in Denmark; So I am Danish by birth. When I was very young, my parents, who then enjoyed a comfortable position, sent me to study in France, where I stayed in a luxurious pension for many years. When I was fifteen, my parents died within a short time, leaving me a considerable fortune, which was managed as guardian by a much older cousin of mine. I have never known exactly what happened, but the result was that in a short time I was in utter misery. Helpless, I then went to ask for protection from some distant relatives, from whom I hoped to receive help in compensation for old favors received from my father. But no one wanted to serve me pretexting various reasons that are irrelevant. I dropped out of school and was able to get a job as a typist in the offices of a wine exporter, whom my family had known for years. He was a good man and he treated me with all consideration, paying me much more than my work deserved and even looking out for my safety with a father's request. But after two years he died too and his heirs liquidated the business. I saw myself on the street again, completely alone. I then went to England, entering the service of an elderly lady, as an escort. She was a bad and selfish woman, whom I had to put up with for a long time, because it was impossible for me to find anything better, all kinds of suffering and insults. Not being able to resist anymore, I left her one day to join the dance group of a magazine company; the salary was ridiculous and the treatment bad, but it allowed me to get out of trouble and I continued to travel through much of Europe. Finally, through some friends, I got a good placement with a lumber company in Capetown, but soon after I got here, the company went bankrupt. By now you know what my job is. Daniel, the nightclub owner, despite his somewhat gruff character at times, is deep down a good person. He pays me more than I can spend, and "concluded Jenny" this is it.

The rest of the way they did in silence. Suddenly the girl stopped.

"I live here," she said. "As you can see, it is a somewhat isolated little house, but it is pretty and has a large garden in the back. I share it with two girls who work in the military hospital of the Navy. Between the three we get relatively cheap.

CHAPTER XI
SUBLIME SACRIFICE

"Jenny! Karl said, taking the young woman's hands in his. "Have you ever been truly happy?

The girl was slow to answer. She finally did, her voice barely audible, her eyes downcast.

"Never! I think never. I only remember being happy when I, as a child, played in the forest of our house in Copenhagen. It is very hard to live alone in the world!

"Yes, Jenny. I know something about what this is.

Her eyes suddenly met his with all the power of fascination that Karl had already observed.

"Tell me, Mr. Morris, what is your real name?

Karl got a lump in his throat.

"I have no other name than this" he assured with little conviction. "My name is Morris, Arthur Morris I am English and my profession is to hunt beasts to take advantage of his skin. I thought I already told you.

"No, my friend" denied the girl. "You are neither English nor a game hunter, nor is your real name Morris. Who are you?

Karl didn't reply.

"Except for the name" continued Jenny, "the other two extremes I know perfectly well. You and your friend are Germans, and your reason for being in Capetown is not to sell furs, but to learn of the movements and intentions of the English.

"You are very intelligent," Karl said wryly. "May I know in what absurd case so big?

"It is not absurd nor is it a free assumption of mine. I just know. I have known perfectly well for a long time what Mr. Andreotti's real work is, even though he does not know that I know his activities.

A spy's cunning may be more than enough to fool a man, but not a woman's intuition. I suspected it right away, especially because of his strong interest in obtaining information from the English officers, and I verified it later. As for you, I knew who you were shortly before I left the nightclub tonight. Your partner's behavior, mainly, gave me to understand; his shock when I named Tony, their crazy hunting stories, their attire, unbecoming to game hunters, their slightly sunburned faces and your knowledge of modern dance, They were more than enough clues to make anyone open their eyes. Later, at Andreotti's house, the few doubts I had left disappeared. Why did you close doors and windows in the oppressive heat tonight? It was an unnecessary precaution to deal with a simple fur sale, don't you think?

Karl had followed Jenny's explanations with a clouded face and a sweaty forehead. A single word from the girl would be enough for him and Helmut to be immediately arrested and interned in a concentration camp. But there was something, something that I couldn't define, that told him that Jenny would never give them away.

"What is your name? "asked the young woman, in German.

"Karl" he said, unable to help it. Karl Weber. You can now notify the police if you wish.

The girl slowly brought her face closer to his. Karl could already feel Jenny's perfumed breath on his face. He automatically circled the young woman's waist, drawing her to himself and joined his lips to hers.

"Karl" Jenny said shortly after, with her head resting on the German lieutenant's shoulder "you must flee immediately; You must both flee, you and...

"Helmut.

"...and Helmut. I'm not the only one who has noticed; also Lieutenant Jenkins suspects something. If you don't, it won't take long for you to be arrested either, and I don't want this to happen, because... I love you, Karl.

He was still around her waist, but his thoughts were very far from there, much further north, in Europe, in Germany. He remembered Naty, his adored Naty. He felt a little guilty. If Naty knew that...!

"We can't leave tonight, Jenny," he said at last. "Surely we are under surveillance, and our sudden departure would fuel suspicion. Tomorrow, on the pretext of going to look for the porters, we will flee.

"And I will never see you again" sobbed the girl. "I have finally found happiness and it passes by my side like a gust of wind.

"Yes, Jenny; we will see each other again one day "Karl assured, not very sure of what he was saying". When this is all over.

"Go, Karl, go right away! "she asked with tears in her eyes." Go with yours and may God protect you.

The girl got rid of his embrace, and opening the door of the house, she disappeared inside.

"Goodbye, Jenny," Karl said. But Jenny couldn't hear him anymore...

On his way back to Andreotti's house, he found him engaged in a series of preparations.

"Thank God you've come back," he said. "With the dawn we must try to flee. One of my men has come to inform me that the English plan to inquire into his true personality tomorrow. I have had three horses prepared to be able to reach the motorboat and with it the "Graf Spee» as quickly as possible.

"Won't you feel like leaving all this? Karl asked. "Here he lived like a prince, his business was flourishing and he lacked nothing.

"Yes, I will feel it in part" answered Andreotti. "But not too much. I have long made up my mind that I will have to leave Capetown one day, and this day has come. On the other hand, I want a little rest, my health is broken by the nervous tension in which I have lived during these last years. I have considerable savings abroad and I intend to use them to spend the rest of my life without worries.

"Where is Lieutenant Berling? Karl asked.

"Upstairs, resting a bit.

Shortly after, Karl reached Helmut, who was lying cross-legged on a bed, calmly smoking a cigarette.

"Don't fall asleep," Karl advised. Within four hours we should be on our way.

"Don't worry, I won't fall asleep. I have had too much coffee and it would be impossible for me. Have you finally left the girl? "Where?

"In her house.

"She is a very pretty girl, but she seems a little dangerous to me.

"Dangerous? Karl asked. "No, she is not. She knows who we are since she saw us. Besides, I have confirmed it.

Helmut jumped up on the bed as if stung by a viper.

"What did you tell her?

"Yes.

"But are you crazy?

"No I'm not. Jenny won't say anything.

"Won't say anything, huh? You've been hitting me all night, for which my stomach still hurts, for little indiscretions of mine, and now it turns out that you tell everything to the first woman who looks at you with cow eyes. It seems like a lie! "Helmut was walking around the room with his hands on his head." What imprudence, my God; what recklessness! These tempestuous passions that you raise wherever you go, will end up being fatal to us.

"Calm down, man! Karl asked. "I assure you that nothing will happen because of her. I'll tell you about Jenny later.

"Later? When? When we're with the water up to the neck? What a nice situation! On one side the English and on the other the jungle with its friendly and unhappy little worms. Anyway, I'm going to have a double cognac to forget. "Helmut disappeared through the door, followed by Karl.

* * *

With the first light of dawn, the two German lieutenants and Andreotti left the city. Their mounts were good and they rode at considerable speed through the thickets and trees of the jungle. Suddenly Andreotti stopped.

"Someone is following us," he said. Let's speed up the march.

They put the horses into a gallop, but frequently had to stop for natural obstacles, such as boggy areas, small streams, or overgrown vegetation.

"Now I'm sure they're following us" Andreotti said again, stopping his mount. From here the horses are no longer of any use. We must abandon them and continue the march on foot.

They shouldered the small bundles the German agent had brought with him and headed into the brush.

After a short while of walking, Karl gave a warning cry. A group of men armed with rifles ran down a nearby hill.

"The indigenous police!" Andreotti exclaimed. "At full speed!

They were about to continue their run when a man appeared in front of them whom Karl immediately recognized as Lieutenant Jenkins. He had a pistol in his hand, with which he pointed it at them, and an ironic smile appeared on his mouth.

"Gentlemen, the comedy is over! "He said". In the name of His Britannic Majesty, give yourself prisoners.

Quick as lightning, Karl drew his pistol and fired almost without aiming. Jenkins put his left hand on his right shoulder and dropped the gun. A new man appeared from the thicket, and taking careful aim, he fired at Karl. But something unexpected, something no one thought of, happened then. A figure, dressed in a white dress, appeared on the scene and flung itself into Karl's arms. The bullet intended for him lodged in the newcomer's back, and Jenny, because it was her, fell to the ground. Andreotti fired his revolver against the one who had wounded the girl, eliminating him with an accurate shot to the head.

Karl knelt beside the young woman and made her rest her head on his arm.

"Jenny!" he exclaimed. "Why have you done this?

"Karl, I... I found out that you were going to be arrested and I wanted to tell you, but... I was late. "She spoke with difficulty, straining enormously, and Karl realized painfully that the girl was dying.

Helmut had a gun on Lieutenant Jenkins, who was leaning against a tree, clutching his injured shoulder with his hand. Andreotti, behind some bushes, watched the indigenous police, who were rapidly approaching.

"Jenny," said Karl, "you have saved my life by exposing yours. You should not do it.

"I'm happy, Karl," she said in a broken voice. "You have given me the only truly happy moments of my life. Now I can say that I have been happy once. "Then she continued": I'm going to die...

"No, Jenny, no! "He yelled, making a move to take her in her arms and lift her up." We will take you with us and you will heal soon.

The girl stopped him with a weak gesture.

"Poor Karl! "She said". You know this cannot be.

The blue color of his eyes became more intense by the moment and his breathing more difficult.

"Karl, tell me something. Over there... in Germany, there is someone waiting for your return... right?

He looked down and felt his eyes cloud over for a moment.

"Is she pretty, Karl? "She asked, stroking the German lieutenant's face.

"Yes, Jenny, she is very pretty; but not as much as you.

"Thank you, Karl" she thanked with a weak smile.

"I wish I could do something for you," he yelled in anguish.

"You can do it if you want. Kiss me one more time.

Karl leaned over the girl and pressed his lips to hers. When he sat up again, Jenny had already expired. Her cheeks were white as snow and her eyes were fixed on the sky.

"Goodbye Jenny! "Karl said, after gently lowering the girl's head to the ground." Never forget you!

At that moment Helmut came running to his friend, and seizing him by the arm, forced him to follow him.

As he passed Lieutenant Jenkins, Karl paused for a moment.

"Do you need something? "He asked.

"Nothing thanks.

"I'm sorry we didn't meet under better circumstances.

Quick as the wind, the three men disappeared into the thicket.

CHAPTER XII
THE ESCAPE

For more than three hours they walked incessantly through the jungle at a brisk pace, closely pursued by the indigenous police. Helmut panted loudly. His lungs seemed ready to burst and his entire body was materially covered in sweat. Without worrying about the possible presence of snakes, which inspired him so much horror, he went into the most colorful undergrowth or splashed without fear in the mudflats and swamps. He was cursing everything under his breath, the English, Karl, the German agent, and himself, and would have rejoiced in part at the appearance of some reptile, on whom he had promised to vent his fury.

Karl, a few steps ahead of his friend, also ran as fast as his tired legs would carry him, barely paying attention to his surroundings. He marched like an automaton, without understanding exactly the reason for that wild flight. Passing a dry, cracked tree, he cut his arm deep with a branch too low, but he hardly noticed. His hands and feet were bleeding profusely and the mud that covered his wounds would have caused a frightening torment to another who had not been Karl, completely oblivious to reality. His attention was focused on the memory of the long series of events that had happened to them in a few hours. His departure from the Graf Spee, the long trek through the jungle on the way to Capetown; the English officers they met in the nightclub, where Jenny had sung for him that song which he thought he was still hearing; the dinner at Andreotti's house and the girl's perfumed breath and, above all, her death in her arms. Karl wondered if it hadn't all been a dream or nightmare from his imagination. But the curses that Helmut was continually muttering behind his back made him desist from such an assumption: it was reality; pleasant and sad reality at the same time.

Andreotti was the only one who kept his cool. Demonstrating great practice, no doubt acquired during his long stay in Africa, he threaded his way through the thick vegetation with relative ease, taking advantage of the most remote paths and finding the most unexpected shortcuts. He occasionally paused for a moment and listened intently, only to immediately resume his dizzying run.

They reached the river where Karl and Helmut had so hurriedly seen each other the previous afternoon.

"These waters are infested with crocodiles," Karl warned Andreotti.

"I know" was his reply. He then removed from a package four small artifacts, the size of an orange, which he carefully placed on the ground.

"Hand grenades" he said, addressing both friends. "This will keep the Saurians away for a few moments. We may draw the attention of our pursuers here, but nothing else is possible.

Andreotti took the four grenades one by one and, after ripping off the safety catch, threw them into the river. Four detonations shook the jungle and as many columns of water rose to a considerable height. Without undressing this time, they immediately jumped into the water, reaching the opposite shore shortly after.

"We have achieved it" said the German agent. walking!

They walked all day, albeit at a slower pace, and by late afternoon they were out of range of the colonial police. Andreotti stopped by some rocks nestled at the foot of a low hill, and shedding his burden, he dropped to the ground.

"We will spend the night here" he said. Within an hour it will rain, and in a storm we would be in danger of getting lost. On the other hand, the three of us are tired and need to eat something and rest for a few hours. With the dawn we will do the rest of the way.

Helmut looked up at the sky. Thick black clouds were gathering by the moment, taking on an extremely threatening aspect. A gale-force wind began to whistle through the trees, whipping violently across his face. His clothes were still soaking wet and he felt cold. He sat next to Karl, who, with downcast eyes, seemed oblivious to everything.

"Come on Karl! Cheer up a bit! "He said". You are not to blame for what has happened. It is convenient that you try to get over it, do not forget that we still have to finish our mission.

Andreotti produced a bottle of cognac from a sack, which he handed to Helmut. He uncorked it and forced his friend to take a long drink. The liquor revived Karl, who immediately seemed to snap out of it. Helmut put the bottle to a severe test, not letting go until his stomach commanded it imperatively.

"Now" said Andreotti "we will look for a cave, abundant in this region, where we can take shelter. The downpour will be big.

After a short search, they found a small grotto, inside which they took refuge. A bolt of lightning, followed by a dazzling light, rent the sky and signaled the beginning of a terrible storm, so frequent in the tropics.

With some dry logs they found they made a fire, to whose warmth they approached. The jungle was silent. Its inhabitants had fallen silent, terrified no doubt by the roar of thunder, and these and the monotonous sound of the thick curtains of water that fell from the clouds, alone disturbed the reigning silence.

"We need to be aware. On these occasions the beasts seek shelter anywhere, and we could have an unpleasant visit.

Andreotti unholstered his revolver, dried it carefully, and loaded it with ammunition taken from a small waterproof canvas case. Karl and Helmut followed suit.

Throughout the night it did not stop raining. With the first light of day they resumed their march, arriving in the early afternoon at the place where they would leave the inflatable boat hidden. But even though they searched everywhere for him, they couldn't find him.

CHAPTER XIII
THE END OF A SPY

"Wow! We just needed this "said Helmut". So, what can we do now?

"Well, reason," said Andreotti in turn. Discuss, to see if we find a way to reach the motorboat.

"I'm pretty sure this was the place.

Karl kept recognizing the shore, pacing incessantly from one side to the other.

"And you are not mistaken," assured the German agent. This past night the sea has been very rough and surely the waves will have broken the mooring and dragged the boat.

"But if we leave it, on land! Helmut protested.

"Exactly where?

"There. Next to those rocks. "Helmut was pointing with his finger at some rocks behind him, about fifty meters from the water.

"Being like this" continued Andreotti, the thing is very clear. The tide has come high, as you can see from the signs left behind, and he has taken it away.

"I ordered the sailors" said Karl "to get as close as possible to the coast. Maybe we can locate them.

The three began to carefully scan the sea. Suddenly Helmut cried out.

"There, there they are. On the right, about two miles from here.

Electively, in the place indicated by Helmut they could see an indeterminate black dot, but logically they assumed that it was the motorboat. They spent more than an hour shouting, gesturing, and waving branches and white rags, but it was all useless. They built a fire, hoping that the smoke would be easily seen by the sailors, but it was not.

"We can't spend all day trying to get their attention. I guess you guys know how to swim, right? Andreotti asked.

"I think it's the only thing I've learned well in this life," Helmut assured.

"Well, let's not waste any more time and try to win the motorboat by swimming.

Andreotti quickly undid the packages he had brought with him and, extracting smaller ones, tied them around his waist, tossing the rest of their contents away.

They jumped into the water and began to swim. They were halfway there when Karl and Helmut's blood ran cold. Andreotti had just let out a cry, a desperate scream, a mixture of fright, pain, and anguish. Karl turned quickly and for a moment he could see the German agent's face twisted into a hideous grimace, before he disappeared under the water.

"Sharks! "Karl said, and immediately began to swim with all his might, following Helmut, who was breaking all world records at the time.

They covered about three hundred meters without being attacked by any shark, and Karl guessed that the one that had torn Andreotti to pieces must have been an isolated specimen. But they did not slow down for that.

"They have seen us, they have seen us! "Helmut yelled minutes later. They come this way.

Shortly after, both friends, helped by the two sailors, got on board the motorboat completely exhausted.

As the "Graf Spee» did not expect them until the following night, they spent the rest of that day and the other sailing around the place indicated by Langsdorff for the meeting, to the great despair of Helmut, who had by then given a good account of the sherry bottle.

At last they spotted a light in the distance that grew larger as it approached, and soon they were on the deck of the battleship, facing Langsdorff, who warmly shook hands with them in welcome.

They recounted in a few words everything that had happened to them since they left the Graf Spee, Karl prudently keeping quiet about Jenny. They also informed the captain of Andreotti's death and its circumstances and informed him of the prompt presence in those waters of a powerful English naval formation made up of the cruiser «Renown», the aircraft carrier «Ark Royal», with sixty aircraft, and four destroyers. Karl also conveyed the opinion of the German agent that the most appropriate thing would be to go to the Indian Ocean, where England did not have powerful units, as well as the presence in Latin American waters of a squadron made up of the cruisers «Cumberland», «Exeter», «Ajax» and «Achilles». Langsdorff sincerely congratulated them on the happy success of his undertaking,

CHAPTER XIV
PERSECUTED

On November 14, the German corsair was already sailing through the Mozambique Channel. He had managed to cross the tip of the Cape of Good Hope without incident, despite the close surveillance that the English established in that area with small-tonnage ships.

The next day a small-displacement ship, the "Africa Shell", was sighted, hit by a torpedo, and quickly sank.

Vice-Admiral Wells learned of the sinking of the «Africa Shell», exactly on the eighteenth, and quickly headed with force «K» towards the Cape meridian with the purpose of intercepting the return of the «Graf Spee» to the Atlantic, since the English commander supposed that, since the corsair ship should soon undertake its return to Germany, that was the only possible way.

The surveillance of force «K» was useless. Due to the bad weather, the aircraft could not take off, and without it it was almost impossible to find the battleship. In view of this, Wells decided to go to Capetown in order to rest his ships' crews, but a few hours after anchoring at the English base, he received news of the sinking of the "Dorio Star", a 1,086-ton merchant ship, by the "Graf Spee», three hundred miles, 270th from the southern border of Angola. The corsair was back in the Atlantic without them having been able to do anything to prevent it.

Wells headed with all his units to a point equidistant from Capetown, Port Stanley and Rio de Janeiro, from which he could rush to wherever the "Graf Spee» was located. But Langsdorff, suspecting Wells's manoeuvre, headed for the South Atlantic, despite the danger of falling under the guns of the South American fleet, less powerful than Force 'K', but a fearsome enemy.

Said South American fleet, commanded by Commodore Harwood, consisted of four cruisers: the 10,000-ton Cumberland, with eight 208-millimeter guns, another eight 102-millimeter guns, and eight 533-millimeter torpedo tubes. She developed thirty-two knots of speed. The "Exeter», of eight thousand three hundred and ninety tons, armed with six 203-millimeter guns, eight 102-millimeter guns, several anti-aircraft guns and eight 533-millimeter torpedo tubes. Her speed was up to thirty and a half knots, little more than the Cumberland. The "Ajax» displaced seven thousand tons and was armed with sixteen cannons, eight of 152 millimeters and eight of 102 millimeters, anti-aircraft and eight 533-millimeter torpedo tubes. The «Achilles» had the same characteristics as the previous one.

In the first days of December, the "Cumberland» was in Port Stanley, carrying out various repairs. Harwood therefore had only the Exeter, the Ajax, and the Achilles, and was forced to keep them far apart to cover a vast area of more than two thousand miles.

On December 3, the commodore received news of the sinking of the «Doric Star» by the «Graf Spee», which was supposed to be in the Indian Ocean. The presence of the corsair in Atlantic waters was later confirmed by the Dutch steamer «Mapia».

Harwood guessed that after the Doric Star was sunk, the German battleship would quickly change position, heading either to the Southwest or to the North. In the latter case, the force «K» would block his path; but if she headed southwest he should meet her with his three cruisers below the Graf Spee. He came to the conclusion that it could appear at dawn on December 12 in the area of Rio de Janeiro; on the afternoon of the twelfth or on the morning of the thirteenth, in the estuary of the Río de la Plata, or on the afternoon of the fourteenth, in the waters of Falkland Island. Where to go? He rightly decided on the central point, that is, the Plata estuary, where maritime traffic was considerable. In a radio message he gave his ships «Exeter» and «Achilles» meeting point for the morning of the twelfth,

Studying the problem carefully, the English commodore came to the conclusion that if the meeting took place before the seventeenth day he would have to face the «Graf Spee» alone, since on the twelfth day the «K» force was still very far away, about fifteen hundred miles from the rendezvous point. Should he just make contact while waiting for the Renown's guns and the Ark Royal's aircrafts? But such contact could be lost at night, and during the day visibility would have to be constantly beyond the range of the corsair's guns. Such reasons made him give up the simple maintenance of contact and decide for combat, skilfully playing the artillery power of his cruisers with their division into three groups, and with their mobility, superior to that of his powerful adversary.

* * *

On December 3, the «Graf Spee» sank the «Tairoa» off the coast of Africa, then heading towards America for two reasons: first, to get away from places where it had been located, and second, because after the sinking of the oil tanker «Ussukuma» by the British, the fuel supply problem had become extremely difficult and the situation was beginning to be dire for the German corsair, who was quickly running out of his last stocks. On the other hand, the English, aware that the steamship «Tacoma», anchored in the port of Montevideo, was loading diesel oil and supplies for the «Graf Spee», was waiting for it at the exit of the Plata estuary.

On the seventh, the pocket battleship hunted down the 3,895-ton «Streonshalm», which it attacked with its two-hundred and eighty-pound artillery, then sailing in the direction of La Plata. On the thirteenth she saw some smoke on her port side, at the limit of the horizon, and she headed towards them to recognize them.

CHAPTER XV
KARL'S SECRET

Since his return to the Graf Spee, Helmut could see a great change in Karl. If he was off duty, he spent most of the day shut up in his cabin or pacing the deck alone and thoughtful. If someone spoke to him, he limited himself to answering with monosyllables or with simple movements of the head. Helmut tried in vain to make his friend react and get him out of the despondency that overwhelmed him. It was true that Karl had always been, or at least as long as he had known him, a bit of an oddball, but lately his strangeness had sharpened considerably.

One night, while the Graf Spee was sailing for America, Helmut went out on deck intending to walk a little before going to bed. The sky was clear and the moon, in all its splendor, was reflected in the slightly rippled sea. A pleasant breeze was blowing, which Helmut filled his lungs with. He leaned over the rail lighting a cigarette.

Five minutes had not elapsed, when a shadow that appeared from the darkness approached him.

"Hello Helmut!

"Good evening, Karl" he greeted.

"Couldn't sleep, huh?

"No. It's too hot.

Both men smoked for a long time in silence. At last Karl, throwing his cigarette into the water, turned to his friend.

"This is getting ugly," he said. We should have been back by now and we are still in the middle of the Atlantic harassed from all sides and without knowing for sure where we are going.

"I trust Langsdorff," Helmut assured him calmly. He will know how to get us out of the jam.

"Langsdorff is not infallible. Without food and fuel, not even he can do anything. Gas-oil is running out at times and howitzers and torpedoes are scarce. Wells and Harwood are closing in on us and they won't be long in hunting us down. It seems to me that the Graf Spee will never return to Germany.

"This is a very pessimistic view of the situation," Helmut said, though he also thought like his friend.

Karl lit another cigarette, and after taking a puff, said:

"I don't know exactly what will happen, but in case things go wrong and I can't go back to Germany, I want you to listen carefully to a story that you will repeat to Naty just as I am going to tell it to you. Then beg him to forgive me.

Helmut made up his mind not to miss a syllable of what he was about to hear. He would finally know the secret that Karl had guarded so jealously for so long.

"I "began his friend", I killed Naty's father.

There was a deep silence that was finally broken by a laugh from Helmut.

"But what nonsense are you saying? Naty's father was torn to pieces by a mine that exploded when the "Staal" was being loaded.

"Exactly," confirmed Karl. I was not the material author, it is true; but that mine was not destined to cause the death of Lieutenant Müller, but mine.

"I don't understand you," said Helmut.

"Now you will understand me. When I was assigned to the "Staal" just after leaving the Academy, I met a lieutenant on that ship, Naty's father, and we immediately became good friends, despite him being much older than me. Müller did not come from the Academy, but he had reached his graduation after long years of service in the Navy. He may have lacked theoretical knowledge, but in terms of practice he gave a hundred and nine to any officer of the current promotions. From him I learned most of the knowledge I have, and it amused him a lot to see how to calculate a simple angle of fire I got involved in complicated mathematical operations that he judged totally unnecessary. He was an excellent person and from the captain to the last sailor he was appreciated and respected. Many years ago he had married a girl, I am referring to Naty's mother, who shortly after came into possession of a large fortune due to the death of her father. Despite the wishes of her wife, Müller did not want to leave the Navy, first because he felt a true vocation towards her and secondly because it did not seem decent to him to live at the expense of money that did not belong to him. Perhaps his judgment was somewhat exaggerated, but he stood firm in his decision.

"At that time," continued Karl, "the Navy did a lot of training, and the Staal, like other ships, spent most of its time sailing. One day, after a long absence, we anchored in a German military port in order to load new material and go to sea the next day. Most of the officers wanted to have a little fun ashore, and with the proper permission of the ship's commander, they scattered about the city. It so happened that precisely that day I was on duty and my mission was to inspect the cargo, ensuring that it was carried out normally. But since work wasn't supposed to start until seven in the evening to finish at midnight, I opted to accompany my friends during the time I had left. We ate in a typical restaurant famous for the quality of its wines, and I abused them. Afterwards we toured part of the city, stopping at as many bars and cafes as we could, and the result was that when it was time to return to the «Staal» to go on duty, I was completely drunk. Naty's father tried to revive me and convince me to leave, since failing to do my job could bring me serious harm, but I insisted, completely dominated by alcohol fumes, to stay with them. I remember that I insulted Naty's father and told him that I would do whatever I wanted. He, taking charge of my state, and so that my absence would not be noticed, replaced me. An hour later, a faulty mine exploded while it was being loaded onto the Staal, killing four men, three sailors and Lieutenant Müller.

Karl fell silent. Helmut watched him breathlessly, a stunned grimace on his face.

"Since then," continued Karl, "I have not been able to get rid of the horrible obsession that I was to blame for his death, that I killed him. The one who until then had been my best companion, he had died horribly because of my unspeakable behavior. The captain of the «Staal» did not find out at the time of the substitution carried out and the other officers who were in on the secret, remained silent. But I couldn't put up with that situation for long and one fine day I went to see Naty's mother and told her everything. I will never forget the effort it took me to finish my story. Mrs. Müller listened carefully to the end without expressing any resentment or emotion. Only deep sadness was reflected on her face. When I finished she told me:

"My son, I don't think you are more guilty than the others. Harold had told me several times about you. He knew that you were good friends and I know that your behavior would have been identical to his in opposite circumstances.

"It seemed to me" said Karl continuing his story "that the weight of a mountain disappeared from my shoulders, that I came back to life. But then Mrs. Müller wanted me to meet her daughter, my friend's daughter, and, bloody irony, I fell madly in love with Naty and she with me. Her mother asked me never to let her daughter know the truth, because, as she believed, it would be more difficult for Naty to forgive me and understand, something of which she was sure, that my behavior was not the cause of her father's death. A few days passed, and disgusted with my cowardice, I appeared before the captain of the "Staal" and told him everything too. I was court-martialed, but a short time later, I still don't know why, the proceeding was shelved and I was reinstated to my post. Since then I have tried many times to get away from Naty, but I have not been able to do it; I love her too much. On countless occasions I have been tempted to tell her the truth of what happened, but the fear of losing her has prevented me. I do not want to continue this farce, and I am determined that you know it and that you judge me as you see fit. I couldn't live by her side with a secret like that between us. But. "Karl stared at Helmut", in case the worst happens and I cannot return to Germany, promise me that you will tell her everything as I have told you.

"You have my word, Karl," Helmut said only.

CHAPTER XVI
BATTLE OF THE RIVER PLATE

In the early hours of December 13, Harwood's division was two hundred miles to the 110th of the Rio Grande do Sul. The weather was good, the sky clear, visibility excellent, a cool breeze from the southeast and the sea slightly lagging in the same direction. At six hours fifteen minutes, the «Ajax» services indicated a smoke in delay 320°. All the twins turned, and the Exeter was ordered to recognize the signal smoke. The commander of said ship informed the commander of the fleet, Commodore Harwood, who was in the «Ajax», that the characteristics of the steamer were those of a pocket battleship. She could not be other than the «Admiral Graf Spee», the dreaded corsair insistently sought after for so many months. The great mass was approaching at considerable speed and the English maneuvered by dividing into two bands. The "Exeter» put her tiller to port to present her starboard side to the battleship. On her side the "Graf Spee» was sailing at 125° and fourteen knots when she recognized the English division at 19,000 meters.

Langsdorff ordered to call to action stations and in a few seconds the corsair ship took an unusual life. Men ran in all directions to take their corresponding positions. The officers distributed the sailors in the appropriate places, and the guns of the three towers began to rotate slowly. The commander of the battleship, realizing that escape was totally impossible, since the enemy cruisers surpassed the «Graf Spee» in speed, prepared to present battle to the three English ships at the same time, fighting on both sides. The wind was favorable to blow away the smoke from the shots and the visibility was magnificent. Langsdorff assigned a 280-millimeter turret to the "Exeter», another to the "Ajax» and the four 150-millimeter guns to the "Achilles».

Four minutes after the sighting, at 4:18 p.m., the «Graf Spee» opened fire on the «Exeter» and the «Ajax» with 280-millimeter guns, at a distance of 18,500 meters. At 6:20 the «Exeter» did it, at 6:21 the «Ajax» and at 6:23 the «Achilles». The commander of the German battleship immediately realized the enemy maneuver, which intended to catch it between two bands, and ordered to concentrate all fire on the «Exeter» to finish it off. The distance had been reduced to 16,500 meters, and the German shot was perfect. The first salvo fell short, the second long and the third forked the ship. The «Exeter» received a real rain of shrapnel that was diminishing its combat capacity at times. At 6:23 a 280-millimeter spike killed all the servants of the torpedo tube assembly, it damaged the transmissions and riddled the funnels and the entire deck. At 6:24, tower B received a centered hit, leaving it out of action, it swept the bridge and only the ship's commander and two sailors were unharmed. Another hit destroyed the rudder and transmissions of the aft command post and only one tower responded to the fire of the German corsair. The captain had no other recourse than to go on deck and direct from the steering hatch by hand the orders to the engines, the artillery and the tubes. At 6:26 another two hits to the bow caused further damage, fires and many casualties. In barely three minutes the "Graf Spee» had disabled the "Exeter» with rapid fire, keeping the "Ajax» and the "Achilles» away from her with her 150-millimeter guns. But at 6:30, Langsdorff ordered the 280's guns to be turned on "Ajax» and the battleship to close in on the light cruiser to destroy it. Until then, she and her twin, the «Achilles» had used sixteen 152-millimeter cannons for only four 150-millimeter cannons, the «Graf Spee»; for this reason, the German commander arranged for a tower of the 280 to be dedicated to them. The maneuver of the battleship put the «Exeter» within the launch zone, which was taken advantage of by the English captain by firing three torpedoes that did not achieve their objective, since that Langsdorff, hiding behind a screen of smoke, easily dodged them.

The "Exeter» received two new hits shortly after. The first destroyed tower A and the second went through the ship, causing large fires inside. By then the English cruiser had both bow towers out of action. All transmissions, mangled. The repeaters of the gyroscopic needle, damaged. Some watertight compartments, flooded. Various fire sources. All torpedoes fired and many dead and wounded. She only had the two aft 203-millimeter guns left, but her effectiveness was almost nil. The fire forced the storerooms to be flooded and the fire to be suspended. Finally, the «Exeter», engulfed in flames, turned to port and abandoned the fight, heading towards the Malvinas, arriving at Port Stanley on the sixteenth.

The «Ajax» then catapulted a reconnaissance plane from the two «Seafox» it was carrying, since one of them was destroyed by shrapnel from the «Graf Spee». At 6:40 am, a strike from the 280 caused great damage to the «Achilles» and the captain was seriously injured. From this moment the German corsair withdrew behind several smoke screens pursued by the English light cruisers, faster and with sixteen 152-millimeter guns, heading towards Montevideo. The English were maneuvering at a distance for fear of the Graf Spee's 280 guns, and there was the biggest clash of the entire fight. The «Ajax» was immediately forked and at 7:24 she moved away from her at full speed, launching four torpedoes to port. At 7:25 a shot from the 280 put the tower X out of action of the «Ajax» and seized the T, not being able to use from now on more than the two bow towers. The reconnaissance aircraft closed in on the German privateer, but was quickly driven away by anti-aircraft artillery fire. The «Graf Spee» was covered again behind a dense screen of smoke, launching at 7:30 several torpedoes that the enemy cruisers were able to maneuver. Harwood then opted to break ballistic contact and get as far away as possible without losing sight of the battleship. His intention was to wait for the arrival of night and under cover of darkness try to approach him and beat him. He had barely started the operation when a hit from the 280 brought down the

Ajax's topmast. At 7:50 the distance between the English cruisers and the «Graf Spee» exceeded 20,000 meters.

CHAPTER XVII
HEADING TO MONTEVIDEO

At eight o'clock on the thirteenth, the «Graff Pee» was sailing at twenty-two knots towards the Río de la Plata, pursued by the English out of the range of the 280 guns. The «Cumberland» was in Port Stanley and the force « K» sailed to Rio de Janeiro to oil and pursue the corsair if he entered the Atlantic. The «Cumberland» was then ordered to join the bulk of the South American fleet and was already sailing at full speed north.

Although the "Graf Spee» had no major damage, and her artillery, engines, and general steering functioned perfectly, fuel was scarce and she had ammunition left for thirty minutes of combat. Food was scarce and some damage had to be repaired, mainly in the kitchens and bakeries, which had been destroyed by the fire of the English cruisers. In such conditions, the "Graf Spee» could not do anything but go to a neutral port and refuel, load supplies and repair damage in accordance with the rules of International Law.

In the early hours of the night the «Achilles» approached the battleship to a distance of 19,000 meters, but two salvos, one short and one focused, from the «Graf Spee» forced it to move away, emitting a smoke screen. Langsdorff ordered that the shots be fired from the bow guns to make the English believe that the stern ones were out of order. The ploy had an effect. Shortly afterwards the "Ajax» and the "Achilles» approached again, being beaten with rapid fire by the stern guns.

At eleven o'clock in the morning an English merchant ship, the «Shakespeare», appeared, but the «Graf Spee» did not sink it, since Langsdorff did not see fit to do so without first saving the crew. The English steamer was saved, therefore, thanks to the noble behavior of the German commander. This one, however, tried to use that encounter to increase the distance between him and his pursuers. For this, he issued a message to the English cruisers in which he said that they pick up the castaways from the merchant ship. But the trick had no effect.

From that moment the English radioed every half hour the situation and course of the corsair, so that the merchants who were in their way could move away at full speed.

At 19:15 the «Graf Spee» fired two salvos at the «Ajax», at 24,000 meters, which were extraordinarily precise, forcing the cruiser to move away quickly.

The La Plata estuary has three entrances. One to the North, between the Uruguayan coast and the English bank. Another in the center, between the English bank and the Ramen bank, and a third to the south, between it and Cape San Antonio. The second is seventeen miles long, and the southern one is forty. Harwood feared that Langsdorff would pretend to head for Montevideo and escape to the high seas by another exit. He made the "Achilles» wait at the North exit and he went to the Central. The South was left unguarded, as the Cumberland had not yet arrived. The «Achilles» was following the battleship, silhouetted by the moon, and decreasing distances as the darkness increased. The English cruiser headed a little towards the NW, to bring the bearing line to the «Graf Spee» to coincide with the azimuth of the sun. At 20:55 the German ship fired on the «Achilles», causing damage and forcing him to hide behind a smoke screen. But the English cruiser had had time to fire as well, responding to German fire, and her hits landed near the battleship's bow tower, without causing serious material damage, but causing some deaths and many injuries. Among these were Karl and Helmut. The first collapsed with a piece of shrapnel embedded in his head and the second was thrown against a steel plate, breaking his leg. Karl, who was lying in a pool of blood, was immediately picked up and taken to the ship's infirmary, revealing a wound very close to his left eye, next to his temple. Helmut had the femur of his right leg chipped in several places and several minor injuries.

Meanwhile, the corsair had come within seven miles of the entrance to the port of Montevideo, silhouetted against the lights of the city. Shortly after he anchored at the docks of the capital of Uruguay and at 11 pm the pursuit ceased.

As the English did not know when the «Graf Spee» would leave the port of Montevideo and there was even the possibility that it would try to do so that same night, they chose not to stay at the outlets of the Río de la Plata, since they were silhouetted against the sky, moving out to sea in search of the "Cumberland», which arrived at twenty o'clock on the fourteenth of December.

When the "Graf Spee» had anchored, Langsdorff arranged for the wounded to disembark, lodging them in a hospital that the Uruguayan Government put at their disposal. Among them were Karl and Helmut.

Helmut's injuries, despite their ostentatious nature, were not serious. Only the broken femur gave any work, but in the end the bones were put in his place, and his leg and part of his body were put in a cast. Karl was something else. The shrapnel had affected various important tissues, also producing abundant tears. At first no one hoped to save him, but little by little hopes grew, until one day the doctor who was treating him declared him out of danger. His friend, who was in a bed next to hers and cared more about Karl's injuries than her own, couldn't hide his joy.

"Is he a friend of yours? the doctor asked him one day.

"Yes.

"Do you know his family?

"It lacks it.

"In that case," continued the doctor, "it is up to you to give him bad news. Your friend will be completely blind.

Helmut felt his body break out in cold sweat. With terribly dilated eyes and half-open mouth, he looked at the doctor as if he hadn't quite understood what he wanted to tell him.

"In a few days," said the doctor, "I will remove the bandage that covers his face. At first he will surely still be able to see something, but soon, before sixty days, he will lose his sight forever. Sorry. It won't be nice for you to tell him."

When the doctor left the room, Helmut leaned back on the pillow and stared at the ceiling of the room. A thousand crazy thoughts crowded disorderly in his imagination.

CHAPTER XVIII
THE END OF «GRAF SPEE»

Langsdorff requested and obtained authorization from the Uruguayan authorities so that his ship could remain for fifteen days, the time he deemed necessary to supply and repair the battleship, in the port of Montevideo. But then, due no doubt to English pressure, a commission of technicians was appointed who ruled that the damage to the Graf Spee could be repaired within seventy-two hours.

When issuing such an opinion, the damage that the battleship had suffered in the kitchens and bakeries, from which a crew of a thousand men had to be fed, was evidently not taken into account. If the international convention of The Hague prescribes that every warship that anchors in a neutral port may be supplied with what is necessary for its navigation, without, however, increasing its combat capacity, and within what a ship can do without increasing said capacity, it is supplying fuel that allows it to reach a port of its nation, evidently within what is allowed, it is also repairing the damages that have occurred in its kitchens and bakeries, without whose operation the crew could not eat or, therefore the ship sail. Despite the efforts made by the German representation, nothing could be achieved, and the "Graf Spee» prepared to load the necessary oil to go to sea. The provisioning work was interrupted several times by the British, but in the end the work was completed.

Langsdorff determined to leave Montevideo on the night of the sixteenth to the seventeenth, since only at night did the Graf Spee have any chance of escaping by outwitting the English cruisers. But the commander of the battleship received a letter from the port authorities informing him that the ship would not be able to leave until the twenty-four hour period had elapsed since the departure of the English merchant ship «Dunster Grageu», which had been made to sea at 6:15 p.m., in accordance with the provisions of article sixteen of the agreement XLII of the Hague Convention. This forced Langsdorff not to leave before 6:15 p.m. on the seventeenth or after 8:00 p.m. on the same day, indicating the time and measure to leave the port in broad daylight. Outside, the «Cumberland», the «Ajax», the «Achilles», the "K" force and the French battleship «Dunkirk», which happened to be in those waters, were waiting for him. Even assuming the Graf Spee managed to break contact with Harwood's ships, the Ark Royal's planes would spot her quickly, and the «Renown» and «Dunkirk» would finish her off. Going out in such conditions meant the destruction of the ship, or, at most, overshadowing the easy English victory with the sinking of some light cruiser.

Then the German legation in Buenos Aires made arrangements so that the «Graf Spee» could, in Buenos Aires itself or in another port, repair damage. But these efforts failed.

As the internment of the ship, in terms of personal safety, was not to the liking of the Third Reich, it ordered that the battleship be blown up. Langsdorff received the order, pale as snow. Surely he would have preferred to die fighting the enemy, than to put an end to the glorious pages written by his ship by sinking it in the greenish waters of the Mar de La Plata. But since his sense of discipline did not allow him to discuss superior orders, he resignedly accepted them and prepared to carry them out to the letter. He ordered that five hundred men be transferred to the «Tacoma», still anchored in Montevideo, and that the rest of the wounded who, due to their light nature, had remained on board, be disembarked. At 18:18 the «Graf Spee» unmoored and left the port followed by the «Tacoma». A few miles away from him,

A tremendous explosion that resounded through space like a cry of pain, shook the German sailors who from the «Tacoma» contemplated the agony of the ship. The battleship listed violently to starboard. Shortly after, another explosion blew out one of the 280-millimeter towers and the «Admiral Graf Spee» sank forever under the waters of the Atlantic. Langsdorff, with moist eyes, greeted for the last time the ship with which he had carried out so many feats on the Ocean in the service of his country, and turning around, he headed in a motorboat towards Montevideo.

* * *

Karl and Helmut were sitting comfortably on their hospital beds. The first one had already had his blindfold removed and, as the doctor told Helmut, he saw relatively well.

"I have to admit that I have been very lucky," he said. "If this piece of shrapnel had hit me two centimeters further back, it would have killed me on the spot.

"Yes, Karl, you were lucky," Helmut said in turn, looking sadly at his friend.

"And how are you?

"Perfectly! " Helmut assured. "Mine doesn't matter.

"I feel like a cloud in front of my eyes," said Karl, passing his hand over his forehead. "It's natural, the wound is serious and I still feel bad about it.

His friend lowered his eyes to the ground, and then, as if making a great effort, he said:

"Hey Karl. You need to know one thing. "Helmut was hesitating, the words were reluctant to come out and he didn't know how to approach the question.

"You will say.

Helmut was about to speak when a nurse entered, followed by Langsdorff. The German captain made a beeline for both friends and held out his hand.

"I have already been informed that you are very much recovered, of which I am very pleased.

They talked for a long time. Finally Langsdorff got up from the chair he was occupying, and turning to both of them, he said:

"Soon you will be repatriated. Our representatives in Uruguay have arranged everything so that the wounded can be sent to Germany as soon as possible. There they will finish healing. "Then, handing Karl a white envelope, he continued: "Please visit my family, you live in Berlin, and your address is on the envelope. Tell them what happened, tell them that I remember a lot about everyone and this letter to my wife.

"Don't worry, my captain, I'll do it that way.

Langsdorff said goodbye to them and headed for the door. He had walked a few steps when he turned slowly and said:

"I am very pleased to have had them under my command. "Shortly afterwards he left the room.

The next day Karl and Helmut found out that Hans Langsdorff had taken his own life by shooting himself in the temple. Guided by a mistaken concept of honor, the one who had so successfully governed the German battleship «Admiral Graf Spee» until then he did not want to survive his ship. Without taking into account that this would improve nothing, because, in addition to moral reasons, the country could demand him greater services in the future.

"We have all lost with his death," Helmut said, intensely affected. "Langsdorff has lost his life, Germany a great sailor and us a good friend.

CHAPTER XIX
RETURN TO THE COUNTRY

The German representation in Montevideo soon obtained authorization from the Uruguayan Government so that the wounded crew members of the «Graf Spee» could be repatriated to Germany. And so, two weeks after the battleship was blown up by her crew, fifty men, including Karl and Helmut, were put on an Argentine steamer bound for Europe.

One morning when both friends were on deck looking at the wake that the ship was leaving behind, it seemed to Helmut that it was the right time to let Karl know of his great misfortune.

"I am happy to be able to return to Germany" he said, to start the conversation in some way, "but I am sorry to leave these seas that hold so many memories for us.

"The same thing happens to me" assured Karl "I will not easily forget all this.

"Do you remember Capetown and the hardships we had fleeing from the English?

"Yes, and from Jenny too. She saved my life at the cost of hers. I will always remember her.

"Hey, Karl," said Helmut then, taking the conversation to the ground he wanted. "Have you noticed discomfort in your eyes again?

"Very often, and more and more," replied his friend, trying to tear off an invisible veil with both hands. "As soon as I get to Germany I will go see a good specialist; I start to be alarmed.

Helmut swallowed hard, opened and closed his mouth several times, and finally realizing that sooner or later he would have to know the truth, he made up his mind.

"The day Langsdorff visited us in the hospital, I tried to tell you something that you have to know, that you need to know. His arrival interrupted me, but now you must listen to me. "Helmut's face was yellow, almost colorless, and his words were uncertain and clumsy. But making a great effort, he continued: "The wound you received on the head is much more serious than you think, Karl.

"Serious, you say? But the doctor assured me that it was not dangerous!

"It doesn't endanger your life, it's true; but the shrapnel affected your optic nerves and before two months... you will have lost your sight. "Helmut's forehead slid large drops of sweat.

"What do you say? "Karl asked, as if he hadn't quite understood.

"You have understood me perfectly, Karl. I'm sorry I had to give you such bad news, but the doctor recommended that I do so on several occasions.

"Does this mean that I will never see again? What will I be blind?

"Unfortunately, it is," said Helmut, laying a hand on his friend's shoulder.

For a moment Karl stood still, like a statue, staring out at the sea. He then slowly turned around and began to walk aimlessly, not knowing exactly where he was going. He then he stopped, raising his hands to his face and, sinking onto a bench against the wall, heaved a sob of despair.

* * *

A few days later the ship anchored in a German port and the wounded were taken ashore and placed in a military hospital. Karl received several recognitions. Helmut still hoped that the Uruguayan doctor had been wrong and that Karl's eyesight could still be saved. But he was soon disillusioned. All the specialists agreed that very soon he would stop differentiating objects and that his vision would soon be totally extinguished, that is, he would be completely blind.

Karl received the diagnosis with complete indifference, which Helmut did not like. If his friend had screamed, or gotten desperate and even if he had cried, his reaction would have had a logical and normal explanation, but that disconcerting silence, that total indifference to his misfortune, scared him.

"You must know how to resign yourself and try to cheer yourself up a little. This is hopeless and nothing can be done "I used to tell you". What is happening to you is very painful and we all understand it. But do not forget that many lost more than you. Remember the companions who are now lying at the bottom of the sea and... remember Jenny too.

"Poor Jenny!" Karl then exclaimed. "How useless was your sacrifice!

"No, Karl, it was not useless. You still have many things left in life, including Naty.

"I don't want to see her anymore! "he said, taking his head in his hands.

"But she doesn't know you're here!" Helmut said. "Anyway, if you're not going to see her, I'll go and tell her everything.

"No!" Karl yelled. "No do not do that. I will go, I promise you, since after all it is necessary. She must know a lot of things and I want to saturate myself with the image of her now that I can still see. Later... everything will be indifferent to me.

Days later, both friends arrived in Wilhelmshaven, returning to travel the same path they had followed a few months before. They were traveling in a car, the same "Mercedes" they had used last time, but this time Helmut was sitting behind the wheel, and Karl, beside him, was looking at the rapidly passing landscape, already somewhat cloudy.

The car stopped in front of the Müller mansion, and Karl, turning to his friend, said:

"You stay here, it will be better.

The joyous sound of the doorbell resounded throughout the house, and almost instantly the door was flung open. Naty's slender silhouette appeared in the doorway, and with a cry of joy she threw herself into

Karl's arms. The girl, still not recovered from her astonishment, laughed and cried at the same time, asking a thousand questions, most of them incoherent.

They entered the house and sat down by the burning fireplace in the living room. It was winter and extremely cold. Karl stared at the flames that devoured the logs stacked on the hearth, realizing to his horror that the glare from the fire barely hurt his eyes.

As Naty's expressions of joy subsided, Karl, forcing the girl to raise her head from his shoulder, stood up.

"Where's your mother? "He asked.

"On the top floor. But leave her now. I want to be alone with you, we'll call her after her.

"Naty" said Karl, "you have asked me so many questions in a short time, that I don't know which one to answer first. But first of all I want you to know one thing. For several years I have desperately fought with myself to make you know something that you do not know, but I have always lacked the necessary courage. On several occasions I have been tempted to get away from you forever, tormented by a secret too terrible for my conscience, but I have not been able to, Naty. However, now I want you to know the truth, something that will surely horrify you, but that you should know, since it would be impossible for me to live by your side if you ignored it any longer. Then judge me as you see fit.

Naty, between intrigued and amused, followed Karl's movements in his nervous walks around the room. At last he stopped and began to speak. His story extended from the moment he met Harold Müller on the cruiser «Staal» until the death of Naty's father. When he finished, the girl, with her face covered, had been crying bitterly for a long time.

Karl went over to her and tried to take her hand, but Naty jerked it away and, getting up, walked away from him in horror.

"And you said you loved me? "She exclaimed with a broken face." And did you have the courage to approach me with lies and falsehoods until you made me fall in love with you? From you... from my father's killer!

Karl took a few steps forward.

"Stay away!" the girl screamed hysterically. "Go, go right now, get out of this house, where you should never have entered!

He understood that Naty's resolution was unbreakable and that he had lost her forever, but he experienced, instead, a peace and serenity such as he had not felt for a long time. He went to the door, took his sailor's cap from a chair, and turning to the girl, who was still sobbing in an armchair, said:

"Goodbye, Natty. I will never see you again.

"I wish so," she added, as Karl opened the door that gave access to the street.

Naty could not suspect then with what tragic exactness her wishes would be fulfilled.

CHAPTER XX
HELMUT SMOKES FOUR CIGARETTES

Some time passed, quite a bit, since Karl left the Müller house, and he never heard from Naty again.

Helmut, for his part, recovered from his injuries, was assigned to the battleship «Von Tirpitz», which he joined after a long leave that was granted to him on his return to Germany. Not for a single moment was he separated from his friend, whom he even took with him when he went to visit his family. Helmut's father, at the request of his son, offered Karl a job in the offices of his artificial silk factory, which he could have performed relatively well despite his blindness, which was by then almost full. But he rejected it, because he understood that the hand that was extended to him was moved by a feeling of pity. He apologized saying that he wanted to rest for a long time and that the pension that he promptly received from the state allowed him to live, if not comfortably, at least without economic hardship.

Helmut's leave ended and he joined his new assignment. Karl lived for some time with the parents of his friend, who were reluctant to let him go. But in the end he did, settling in a modest boarding house in Nuremberg, according to his means.

Meanwhile, Naty, who was unaware of Karl's sad condition, made an effort to relegate everything related to him to oblivion, without success. She over and over again she mentally repeated each and every one of the words that the boy used to narrate the events that occurred several years ago, and that cost her father her life. She was trying to find a justification for Karl's behavior, something that would excuse him, or at least lessen his fault, and at the same time convince her that what had happened was nothing more than chance, a horrible chance. But with this she did not achieve anything other than to enlarge in her eyes the guilt of the man who caused that misfortune.

One day when the girl was sitting on a bench in the garden of her house, lost in thought, her mother approached her.

"Naty" he said, "I've been wanting to talk to you for a long time. What really happened between you and Karl?

She, who had given her an explanation different from the authentic one, ignoring that her mother had known the truth for a long time, answered:

"Now you know. Karl and I didn't hit it off. Our way of being was very different and, when we realized it, by mutual agreement we decided to separate. This is all.

"Naty" Mrs. Müller continued, "I have been watching you carefully and I can assure you that something is wrong with you. You are constantly sad and down and I have seen you cry numerous times. When I talk to you, either you don't answer me or you seem to wake up from a deep sleep. What did Karl tell you the last time he came to see you?

"Nothing, mom. You know what happened, and...

"Karl told you something that happened many years ago, when he was serving on the «Staal» cruiser with your father, right?

The girl could not repress an involuntary movement of surprise.

"He did not "weakly assure", he told me nothing about that.

Mrs. Müller sat next to Naty and took her hands in hers.

"My daughter," she said, "I think you have judged Karl's fault too harshly.

"But, mom, do you know...?

"Yes, daughter, I know. I've known for a long time. Karl himself told me everything a few days after it happened.

"But how could he dare...?

"Listen to me, Natalie. Karl came to see me and, as I told you, he told me everything. I knew that your father and Karl were good companions, despite the age difference between them, and the spontaneous confession he made to me was enough to understand that Karl couldn't justly be blamed for something that nobody caused. Karl had drunk excessively, in the company of your father and other officers, and the state in which he found himself did not allow him to reason and understand the consequences that his behavior could have. Your father, because of the friendship that united them, wanted to avoid a possible disappointment and offered to replace him, but otherwise, Karl would have proceeded in the same way. Nobody can be blamed for the rest, it was a fortuitous event arranged by providence, and it is not fair to pretend to see Karl as the person responsible for it. On the other hand, Was Karl's behavior worse by abusing the drink, or that of the others by allowing it? No, Naty, you have judged the case from a false point of view.

"But, mom!" Then the girl said. "Have you forgiven him?

"Yes, Natty. I forgave his little fault right away. Karl has suffered a lot, and for all these years your father's death has been a continual obsession with him. He has always believed himself more responsible for his death than he really is.

"If he told you everything, why did he hide it from me?" Naty asked.

"Because I asked him to do so," said Mrs. Müller, smiling. "I knew it would be more difficult for you to understand, but apparently he couldn't hide it from you any longer. It is one more proof of his nobility and his sincere repentance.

"What consequences did it have for him from a career point of view? the girl asked.

"He was court-martialed, because, despite the fact that his companions were silent, he brought it to the attention of the captain of the «Staal». However, I managed to have the procedure dismissed and he was reinstated in his position. Your father would have wanted it that way.

Naty threw herself crying into her mother's arms.

"I have been stupid! "She said between sobs." Now I understand everything, now that I have lost him forever.

"No, Naty, you haven't lost him," Mrs. Müller denied. "Karl loves you very much, and if you go looking for him you will end up reconciling.

So the girl did. She for a long time she searched for him in vain throughout Germany. She visited his former classmates, but none of them knew how to tell her about Karl, nobody knew where he was. She talked to Helmut's parents, since he was absent, and they couldn't guide her either. In the official organizations from which Karl received his monthly pension, they told him that it was sent to Lieutenant Helmut Berling, because the interested party had so arranged, and that he handed it over to him. In this way another year passed without Naty's hopes diminishing.

One day when the girl was walking along the Under der Linder in the company of a friend, a group of Marine officers crossed her path and she cast her eyes absently for a moment. She stopped suddenly, for she had just recognized Helmut. The boy was chatting animatedly with his companions and did not notice her. Naty ran to meet him, taking him by the arm. Helmut turned quickly and stared at her with a cold expression.

"Hello, Naty! "He said". What a surprise!

"Helmut," she exclaimed pleadingly. "Where is Karl? I need to know it.

"You surprise me, Naty! "he assured with a cynical smile. "What do you want to know about Karl?

"I want to ask you to forgive me for my foolish behavior," she said. "I never thought I could be so unfair to him!

"And this, Naty, couldn't you understand it before? "Helmut asked. "Don't you think it's a little late already?

"No, Helmut, it's not too late, it can't be! I love Karl more than ever and I'm sure he loves me too and he will know how to forgive me. When I learned the truth, I couldn't react any other way, but since then I've had time to reflect slowly and...

"Hey, Naty" Helmut said, softening the tone of his words. "No one can blame you and neither can I. It was hard to guess that such a thing could have ever happened, and your reaction was partly natural and logical. On this side there is no impediment to your returning to Karl, since he has never taken your behavior into account. But there is something else, Karl is no longer the same as before.

"This does not matter. I will get him back to being the one you and I knew.

"He's blind, Naty.

"This doesn't matter either. I am convinced that he will understand that I...

"No, Naty" interrupted Helmut, with a bitter smile. "I don't mean that kind of blindness, but quite another. Karl is blind in the most literal sense of the word, he can't see, do you understand?

A terrible convulsion ran through the girl's body. As if she couldn't understand what Helmut meant, she slowly raised a hand to rest against her right cheek. Her lost eyes stared without seeing.

"Blind? "She murmured.

"I'm sorry I had to cause you this pain" said Helmut, grabbing Naty by one arm, because he feared that at any moment she would collapse to the ground. "A piece of English shrapnel embedded itself in his head, next to his temple, engaging his optic nerves. When he went to see you he still saw something, a little, but it was not possible for him to distinguish the objects and some of their details. He told me that he wanted to engrave you in his imagination before...

Naty, a woman in love after all, did not know how to react to her pain except with tears, although in this case justified in part, and between sobs she hid her face against Helmut's chest, who, frightened, did not know which side to take part.

* * *

Karl had settled, according to his means, in a modest boarding house in Nuremberg. Except for Helmut, no one had been made aware of his residence. He did not give up and hoped to be able to accommodate his life to the new conditions that fate had given him, but as long as he did not get a little used to his new existence, he preferred to stay away from everything that related to his past. was related.

His first intention was to try to forget what was left behind, and to get used to the idea that a new life was beginning for him, to which he had to adapt until he could manage with relative ease. But although he was slowly getting the last, it was not possible, on the contrary, to erase the memories of his previous existence. On his long walks around Nuremberg, which he already knew by heart, and during the nights that he stayed awake for long hours, a long series of familiar images were cited in my imagination, giving life to past episodes, in which he had played a leading role. At first, these memories bothered him and he tried to push them away, but soon he realized that his evocation was the only source from which sprang the most pleasant moments of that inner world in which he was locked up. Countless times he relived the odyssey of the "Graf Spee» since he left the lands of his homeland, until he disappeared swallowed by the waves of the Atlantic, going through each and every one of the vicissitudes he had to go through on his long journey. Helmut and the other companions of the battleship corsair, its commander, the unfortunate ship's captain Hans Langsdorff, and Naty, who could not forget for a single moment, occupied a preferential place in his recollections, also leaving a preferential place for Jenny, the beautiful girl who wanted to sacrifice her life to save Karl's.

One day when he were walking through a small garden that the boarding house where he was staying had in the back, he was told that a Navy lieutenant wanted to see him. He guessed at once who it was, and, with great joy, ordered the visitor to be brought to where he was.

Shortly after Helmut hugged his friend and he could hardly contain the emotion. They sat down on a wooden bench, while, a few steps behind, Naty looked at Karl through the tears that covered her eyes.

"How glad I am to see you again! Helmut said to his friend. "You have to tell me many things. How do you distribute the time? What do you use it for?

Karl gave him a quick summary of his activities, detailing how he was slowly getting used to his new life.

"And you? How does your present destiny test you?

"Very well, Karl. Ah, the «Tirpitz»! What a ship! If Langsdorff had had it instead of the «Graf Spee», he could have laughed at the "K" force and the whole division of South America. "Then, changing the tone of his voice, he asked: "Don't you think, Karl, that you live here very alone? Why do you insist on getting away from the world in which you have always lived and from all those who appreciate you?

"It's better this way," said Karl. In that world to which you refer there is no longer a place for me. I am nothing more than a poor useless, a hindrance...

"You're wrong, Karl" denied his friend. "You will only be a hindrance to the extent that you want to be. It is a mistake to believe that a simple physical injury, however annoying, can put an end to a whole life. You have left many things behind you and you don't need to live the rest of your existence only on memories, you still have real things at your fingertips.

"No, Helmut. It is better to leave things as they are. I am getting used to the idea that everything has been a nightmare and that the only reality is this. It is true that on many occasions I cannot avoid remembering the past, mainly some of its aspects, and I do not dislike reliving it, but I still do not know if the one who manages to save some memory or the one who loses them all is happier.

Naty had been following the conversation between the two men with bated breath and great anguish reflected on her face. Helmut got up, and putting a hand on the shoulder of his friend, said:

"Now that I remember: I have to pay for the taxi, which must still be waiting at the door. I'll be right back. "With a quick step, he walked away.

Karl was left alone, or so he thought. He leaned back on the bench, awaiting Helmut's return, and without much difficulty lit a cigarette. In a little while he thought he heard footsteps, very faint and muffled, on the gravel of the garden.

"Is that you Helmut? "he asked.

No one answered. Now he was sure that he clearly perceived slow footsteps very close to him. There was no doubt that someone was approaching, and Karl, with his head turned to the side from which the noise had come, tried in vain to penetrate the darkness around him and check who he was.

"Are you back yet, Helmut? "he asked again. But this time, too, he received no answer.

With a sixth sense he felt the proximity of a body and, shortly after, the touch of a soft hand on his own. He jerked as if shaken by an electric shock and tried to get up, but couldn't. Two arms had wrapped around his neck, and almost at the same time, he felt the sweet pressure of lips on his. Then a voice that was very dear to him sounded close to his ear like a whisper:

"Karl, forgive me.

"Naty! "He was still able to mutter, before surrounding the girl's waist.

Helmut finished his fourth cigarette and, stubbed it out against an ashtray, prepared to return to Karl. Maria, the owner of the pension, came out to meet him.

"Will you spend the night here? "She asked.

Before answering, Helmut took a few steps, stopping before a large window that overlooked the entire garden. Then, with a wide smile on his lips, he turned slowly.

"No, Maria" he said. "Also, I am sorry to inform you that you have lost a good client. Help me pack Mr. Weber's bags, we're all leaving today.

And he started walking towards Karl's room.

END